MW01114114

Phase One After Zero

Phase One After Zero

A Novel by
Vladimir Chernozemsky

Triumvirate **P**ublications
Los Angeles, California

Phase One After Zero
by Vladimir Chernozemsky

Published by: Triumvirate Publications
497 West Avenue 44
Los Angeles, CA 90065-3917
Phone/Fax: (818) 340-6770
E-Mail: Triumpub@aol.com
Web: www.Triumpub.com
SAN: 255-6480

Copyright © 2005 by Vladimir Chernozemsky

This is a work of fiction. All incidents and dialogue, and all names and characters with the exception of some well-known historical and public figures, are products of the author's imagination and are not to be construed as real. Where real-life historical and public figures appear, the situations, incidents, and dialogues concerning those persons are entirely fictional and are not intended to depict actual events or to change the entirely fictional nature of the work. In all other respects, any resemblance to persons living or dead is entirely coincidental.

All rights reserved. No part of this publication may be reproduced, stored in a retrieval system, or transmitted in whole or in part, in any form or by any means, electronic, mechanical, photo-copying, recording, or otherwise without the prior written permission from the author, except for the inclusion of brief quotations in a review.

ISBN: 1-932656-03-0

Library of Congress Control Number: 2005902951

First Edition. Printed in the United States of America
0 9 8 7 6 5 4 3 2 1

Cover and Page Design by Carolyn Porter
        One-On-One Book Production, West Hills, California
Production: Nancy Gadney
Editing: Carolyn Porter, Steve Hobson

Dedication

To my dear factotum and friend,
Alan Gadney.

The Author

FROM THE AUTHOR

What attracted my attention to this specific idea were cutouts from old newspapers. As an avid reader of magazines and newspapers, my deceased wife cut out coupons, interesting facts, stories and pictures, then stashed them away like a squirrel...

Several years after her passage, I found her trove neatly stored in files. One of the newspaper clippings was about Timothy McVeigh, the notorious Oklahoma City Bomber. The article contained someone's statement that Timothy had actually escaped capture and joined a terrorist group in the Middle East. These types of preposterous stories, as we all know, keep appearing every day, seemingly now more than ever. Just look at the newspaper racks in your grocery store.

I said to myself, "If this were to *really* happen...it could have only happened in another reality, a parallel dimension."

But then I found more. Next to an advertisement for a miracle cure for hair-loss, sat an obscure article about the Oklahoma Murderer's twisted romance with a crazy Canadian girl: There was a bungled miscarriage and she died in the hands of a non-licensed practitioner. According to the article, the bogus doctor then chopped the bodies of mother and fetus to pieces and buried them in different locals so that no remains were left.

And later there was another clipping concerning the same young woman. In this version, she was sired by members of an underground Communist cell, went through drug rehab, became a patient at a psychiatric clinic, and was eventually transferred to a state loony house for the rest of her life. Now these stories of McVeigh's girlfriend didn't necessarily have to happen in a parallel reality (they happen here all the time) — though I did find another McVeigh tale that was certainly of the paranormal.

In this news story (based on his own diaries) a UFO brought McVeigh to Earth from another world (I'll call the planet "Vegha 77"), and his eventual departure from Earth, after the Federal Building Bombing, back to where he came from, was even witnessed by an FBI agent... The agent also discovered McVeigh's original diaries, sold them to a private collector, and now they have disappeared from sight. Uh, huh... And sworn testimony from the FBI agent about McVeigh's "space connection" is now also permanently hidden in the basement of the National Archives.

Wow! All of this *had* to be placed in a parallel reality.

What's baffling to me about parallel dimensions is that the possibilities are countless. Which reality-zone is the original, and which are just reflections. What we think of as our life on planet Earth, the people and the places, could be just reflections in parallel mirrors, where history changes, takes different paths, or maybe is simply postponed and eventually arrives at the same outcome because the course of history may be irrevocable. It's possible we all exist only in our mind's eye and the rest is fiction.

B-u-u-urrr—spooky. We may be, twins, triplets and so forth, the universe is the limit. We may die on planet Earth, but how about the *other* guys, who could be more genuine than us. Is your "original" held as a hostage in a distant universe or maybe in the Hands of God?

Can we correct history, the past, present and future in other dimensions, where possibly rather than "Good over Evil" it's "Evil over Evil" — where maybe McVeigh's type of evil can defeat the other "Evil" that happened 9/11?

In this novel I am trying to explore some of these possibilities.

Vladimir Chernozemsky

Phase One

Gregory MacPherson felt nothing, except the animalistic instinct to escape. Before he set off the blast, he had paid the motel bill with a phony credit card. His clunker Chevy Marquise started faithfully, all cylinders rhythmically engaged—nothing faulty. Before dropping him off at the motel, Larry had driven him by the ruins of the City Hall. For a few moments Greg considered driving by again, but his gut instincts told him to make tracks. The two Arabs from #12 left their room, obviously puzzled at the sounds of nearby explosions. MacPherson laughed inwardly. They should be, he thought. He drove slowly out of the parking lot. The emergency sirens screamed incessantly.

Time didn't matter to him, only distance. There was nothing to worry about, except changing his license plates. He had a stolen pair and had phony papers to go with them. His spare tire was no good, but Canada wasn't that far. He drove according to the posted speed limit, respecting all signals. The city traffic was erratic, though once on the freeway, there were hardly any other vehicles.

Greg reached toward the radio, then withdrew his hand. He wasn't interested in someone else's perceptions.

Everything went according to his master plan. He was a *Force of One*, except for Larry. But Larry was nothing. It was Gregory MacPherson against *them*.

The day was great. He washed every single thought out of his head. Through the open window, the air rushed at his chiseled face, roughing his cropped hair. What a feeling to be young and powerful!

A hitch-hiker. Sorry, no company. Ten miles further, he spotted a rest area. It was empty. He parked his car, opened the trunk and changed into a pair of running shorts and a jersey top. He felt good—strong and perfect. He whistled as he changed the license plates.

What else? The windshield was dirty because the automatic washer didn't work. He cleaned the window with paper towels and water, then looked underneath the car. Something was making a clinking sound—the exhaust pipe had become loose again. His heightened senses alerted him to someone or something close by. He looked up.

It was a police cruiser. "Hi, guys," his cornflower-blue eyes were smiling.

The cop on Greg's side pushed his hat to the back of his head and turned down the police radio. "Need any help?"

Greg sat on his rump. "Not really, officer. It's just an old clunker."

The officer listened a bit to the radio. "Coming from the city?" he asked.

Greg feigned naiveté. "No. From the farm over there. Why?"

The man adjusted his sunglasses against the glare. "No TV?"

Greg shrugged his muscular shoulders. "I'm just a lowly hired hand. Now here, then there...."

The driver interrupted. "Where is there?"

"I'm just out of the Marines and traveling around for awhile," Greg answered.

The sergeant impatiently turned to the officer at the wheel. "Let's go."

The police car pulled away, tires screeching. The officers hadn't asked for identification. That should've been done before anything else. Later, they explained that the guy didn't look like a murderer.

What are murderers supposed to look like?

Greg sat behind the wheel laughing. He checked the gas gauge—plenty to get where he was going. He referred to the Triple A map to double check his route. He drove to a parallel road, careful not to speed—speed attracts attention. Obviously, he hadn't been identified—yet. The license plate number written in the motel's registration book was different from what he had now. Besides, if the police checked that motel, the detectives were most likely to focus on the obvious—the Arabs.

Greg stopped for a meal and coffee. He tipped the waitress generously. Would she come along for a quick fuck? he thought to himself. No-o-o…she might remember his face. He shouldn't push his luck too far. His sexual urge blurred his mind.

He drove to a secluded place and parked. There, he relieved himself of his sexual tension and felt a sense of release. Life in a Marine barracks had taught him well.

Now he was able to think straight. Back on the road he was more able to concentrate on driving. He found the freeway that led to his destination. More traffic…so what?

Greg drove well into the night, stopping only in the wee hours to sleep in the car. At sunrise, he woke up refreshed, walked into the brush and relieved himself. As he zipped up, a friendly puppy appeared from nowhere. He played with it for awhile, then shooed it away. He had no need for companions.

Greg bought coffee and donuts and ate while driving. He disposed of the remnants through the window.

Before long, he pulled into a gas station and parked his old car in a spot next to an even older Mercedes with a "FOR SALE" sign attached to the back window. While buying some snacks and drinking water, he glanced at the newspaper's headlines. He saw nothing pertaining to him. The Arabs were mentioned at the bottom of page one, and there was also a short interview with the motel clerk, "Yes, there was a young man, very polite and quiet." Then a description of his car, coupled with the true license plate number. "Shucks…" muttered Greg. There were two TVs on in the shop, and a single sales person was looking at to one of them, paying little attention to him.

Greg went out and checked the Mercedes. It wasn't locked. He got in and looked around. The keys were behind the sun visor. He removed his Chevy's stolen plates, threw them into the Mercedes and shifted the "FOR SALE" sign onto his old car. A lady drove her car up to the high-test pump as Greg slid behind the Mercedes' wheel. He was lucky. Now, would it start? It did and it sounded better than his old car. He left through "EXIT ONLY." The windshield wipers didn't budge, but the weather was in his corner. Everything else seemed in perfect working order, including the radio.

However, the gas gauge showed nearly empty. Greg drove to the next gas station, filled up and paid with cash. He pumped some air into the worn-out tires. Bad news—they didn't look too good, but he had to take some chances. It was the story of his life.

By the end of the day the weather changed abruptly. The young fugitive sniffed rain in the air without needing a weather forecast. He again stopped to get the wipers repaired, again paying cash.

When Greg had set his master plan in action, to blow up the city hall, he had made certain he had an escape route. He had the phone numbers and addresses of three "friendly" cells, one in Minneapolis and two in Canada. Greg didn't trust telephone lines. He felt strangely disaffected from his own security. There was no one he knew in the underground, except for Larry, who he had never cared for. Larry was trustworthy to a certain point, but probably a latent homo. Neither one of them belonged to a cult. Both shared pot, but never sentiments. They lacked any common interest save for explosives and detonators. Both were tacit and reticent by nature. At times, Greg found Larry despicable, a mama's boy who fed on books and propaganda. At times, they hated each other.

It didn't matter. Nothing mattered anymore except his own escape. He was on the run, but at least his escape route was laid out.

For the moment he was rather impressed with himself. He had accomplished his plan of blowing up the establishment who didn't believe he was capable of even risking his life for them in exchange for meager pay while he was in the Marines. Now those saps will see who Gregory MacPherson is!

One

Gregory MacPherson abandoned the Mercedes just before crossing the Canadian border, undetected, at an unguarded area he was previously told about. Now, on foot, he made his way north. Mother Nature had endowed Greg with good night vision, and he had been trained by the Marines to endure extreme cold and heat (as well as learning hand-to-hand combat). Barefoot, clad only in shorts and shirt, he had his clothes and shoes in a water-resistant package along with his false identifications and a small amount of Canadian currency. The darkness was soothing to him. His military wristwatch/compass was readable and told him his whereabouts with precision. He carried a miniature flashlight and map for reference. Greg remained favored by the weather, and his presence was still undetected.

Greg approached the designated house in a roundabout way. The dogs had been taken inside. Someone calmed them. The night was fading into a grayish morning fog that crept low to the ground. Greg shed his wet wear and dressed in the woodshed. The smell of chopped wood reminded him of a boyhood on a ranch in the Rockies. Most of his memories were unpleasant. He shook them away. He had to keep a clear mind.

Greg's first objective was to establish contact exactly as had been planned. Catlike, he walked to the door and knocked out the code. Light came on almost instantly. The door cracked open. A crisp male voice came from behind:

"Where did you come from, stranger?"

Greg uttered the code word, "Titicaca."

"Are you the thin man?" the man retorted.

"No," Greg answered like an automaton. "I was made in Waco, Texas."

The man ushered him in with some reluctance. "I might be under surveillance, but I'll drive you to the city. Do you have the address?"

"Yes, sir."

The man looked at him in the glare of a bright light. "Let's go."

The truck was new, though nothing fancy. The owner held the door open for Greg, then banged it shut. He went back into the house, set loose two vicious Dobermans, then leaned on the door, munching something while sipping from a coffee mug.

Greg was hungry and thirsty. But the Canadian, who sported a curly beard and mustache and a large beer-belly, didn't offer Greg anything. He ate in full view of him, perhaps just to parade his negative feelings.

Greg got the message. He tried to pretend it made no difference to him. The fog lifted, but the rain started again. To make matters even more uncomfortable, Greg's host was a chain-smoker, and there was no ventilation. The driver insisted on keeping the windows shut. He didn't bother to introduce himself and Greg followed his example. No other names were mentioned. The city was "the city," the mountain, "the mountain." The radio was silent, but the man whistled out of tune. Greg found a last chocolate bar in his bag and ate it slowly, making him even hungrier and thirstier to a murderous point. The man weighed at least two hundred fifty, his narrow eyes lost in fat, and he had large, pudgy hands. He stunk of sweat and dirty underwear.

Greg was mad. "I could take him down instantly," zipped through his mind, "but not now. The damn sadist—I'll find a way to pay him back." Greg glanced murderously at the insensitive slob.

They passed several eating places. The younger man glared again at his host, but said nothing. In the next hour this shit-bag was due to get hungry no matter how much he stuffed himself. And what city were they headed for? Greg knew the address, but for security reasons, not the name of the city.

The city was Hamilton, the address was a high-rise condominium building on the outskirts. MacPherson was glad to part with the hostile farmer. Not a word was spoken, but surely a lot of curses crowded both their minds. Greg slammed the truck door with a bang, making a mental note to find this prick sometime in the future and teach him some manners.

The truck revved away. It was past noon and the hunger pangs in Greg's stomach gnawed at him. There was no sign of any eating place. He braced himself, crossed the lobby and took the elevator to the sixth floor. The name on the door corresponded to the one in his instructions. A girl in her teens answered the bell. She scrutinized him head to toe.

"My father isn't home. You may find him at his repair shop." Then, as if she had a change of mind, "Are you by any chance Armando?"

Greg offered the stolen driver's license with a retouched picture. The girl looked at it carefully, then back at the original.

"You don't look Latino, but come on in. I'll call my dad." She dialed a number, then spoke in French. After a short exchange, she handed him the receiver.

"Are you looking for a job?" croaked the voice.

"Not really," Greg answered. "I'm on vacation."

"I'll be home shortly."

Greg set the receiver in its cradle. He needed a shave. The girl pointed at the bathroom.

"You can use my dad's electric razor. Would you like a drink?"

Greg turned from the bathroom door, "How about a cup of black coffee and some food? I missed my breakfast."

The girl smiled for the first time. She was pretty by any standard and she reminded him of someone. "When you're finished shaving, sit at the dining room table. You can switch on the TV." She then busied herself in the kitchen.

Greg felt fresher after his shave. He sat at the table, but didn't turn on the TV set. He devoured the food with relish, and the young girl refilled his coffee cup twice.

As he munched on the buttered toast, Greg asked, "By the way, what's your name?"

"Lydia," she informed him with a smile.

He continued staring at her, saying, "That's a pretty name."

"Are you really Armando?" she asked coyly.

Greg shook his head. He felt comfortable and welcome. "Does it matter? What do you do all day?"

She giggled, "I go to school, then make up stories with my puppet theater. The funny thing is, my favorite character in my puppet theater is Armando."

"Well, then," Greg teased her, "I'll have to be Armando."

Lydia shook her head decisively, "I don't think you look a bit like an Armando."

"Aren't you a little too old to be playing with a puppet theater?" Greg asked, beginning to enjoy their conversation—something he hadn't done for awhile.

Lydia's dark eyes became very serious, almost tragic. "That's what mother used to tell me. She didn't know me very well. My father, Ian, agreed with her, but he knows me better...people say I am mad. At times he even participates in my charades—doing the voice of Armando. But he makes Armando sound like a child, and Armando is full grown. Anyway, I don't want to grow up. I'll just become older and older...then die."

Greg shrugged. "We all die sooner or later, Lydia."

The girl pierced him with eyes full of premature knowledge, then uttered in a very low voice, "During her last pregnancy, mother's health deteriorated considerably. She was getting too old. She lost the babe at seven months—it was a baby boy."

Lydia then added, "Strangely, somehow I feel my baby brother's presence."

What do you mean, is he a ghost?" asked Greg.

"Not really, but I see him growing up," Lydia asserted calmly.

"Does your mom feel the same?"

The girl's voice became very small, almost inaudible, "Mom passed away almost six years ago. Do you want to die sooner?"

Greg was taken aback, "I haven't thought about it, though I guess I've been playing with death since I remember." He stopped talking for a short while, then he said seriously, "How does it feel to be crazy Lydia?"

The girl smiled in a forlorn way. "Sometimes I think differently than other people."

Greg sat back in his chair. "Everyone thinks differently—at some time." Then he changed the theme abruptly, "Hey why don't you show me your puppetry while we wait for your father."

The broom closet was her puppet stage. Lydia was in the process of explaining and showing Greg her little puppetry center when her father arrived.

He seemed deeply preoccupied. He kicked the door to her stage shut along with her dolls. He then, sent Lydia to her room and faced Greg with not a trace of sympathy. "Okay, young man, what do you want of me?"

Greg sat down at the table and pushed the food tray aside. "I thought you were given instructions."

His host nervously lit a cigarette. "What you did isn't what I bargained for. You acted on your own."

"But I was given your address," the younger man smiled pleasantly. "I thought you were alerted to my coming."

The other man let the cigarette smoke stream from his nostrils. He lowered his voice. "Do you realize the scope of your heinous act and its repercussions?"

Greg's smile became brazen. He placed his elbows on the table and held his square chin in his cupped hands. "You tell me."

The host felt like punching this wise ass, but Greg anticipated him. "I wouldn't start a fight if I were you. It will upset your daughter, it's bad for her nerves. You don't want to involve her, do you?"

The man held his piston-like fists by his thighs. "I want you out of here! You don't even belong to the human race."

"The human race doesn't belong to me, either." Greg snarled. "I just treated the system like its been treating me."

"You could be replaced, young idiot," the man shouted. "The people you killed are irreplaceable."

Greg tried to argue, "The people murdered in Waco…

"Were killed by fanatics like you!" the man finished his sentence. "I had a niece in that cult. Now get out of my flat. Find your own way to hell!"

Gregory MacPherson glanced at the broom closet as if to say adieu. The door had crushed in the chest belonging to the puppet Armando. Only his left hand and smiling ruddy face had somehow been spared.

Gregory MacPherson didn't use the elevator. He made it down the steps as he tried to collect his thoughts. He shouldn't have counted on Larry's connections to the underground. They were soft characters, like Larry. Greg again thought of himself as a one-man army. He should always depend on his own resources. The day was unusually cold, and he had lost his army jacket. Would it lead to his capture? Perhaps, but not in Canada.

He had never been to Hamilton. That girl could've helped him around the city. Well, no chance. Except for escaping, he hadn't planned what he would do after "zero." His only thought at the time was to destroy what he hated—the system and everyone in it. The contacts and the money were Larry's provision. Larry engineered the escape route, and now that escape route wasn't all it was supposed to be.

Everything had gone down the gutter. Gregory MacPherson was just another fugitive. It started raining again. The people around him had umbrellas and raincoats. Greg had his hands in his pant's pockets, shoved deep, trying to keep warm. He found shelter in the entrance of a movie theater then spotted a public telephone. That girl had a name. What was it? Something different… Lin…Lydia. Yes, he had the phone number. Her father must've gone back to work. She might be home alone.

At the phone booth, Greg pulled some change from his pocket, then dialed. The girl answered. He felt relieved—almost joyful.

"Hey, Lydia, it's me…remember, Armando? I left without telling you how appreciative I was of someone cooking a meal for me, how much I enjoyed the puppet show. Those nice things don't happen everyday—for me. Hello—Hello! Are you there?" He hung on to her invisible presence as he would to a life jacket in the high sea.

Finally Lydia answered haltingly. "Yes, I'm here. Where are you?"

"At the entrance to a movie theater, sort of lost. I have to buy a jacket." The street noise rose, he covered one ear, "Hello, Lydia, don't hang up, please. I have no one else to ask…hello?"

She came back as from another world. "I hear you, but I can't help you."

"Why, Lydia? Just tell me how to get to a store for second-hand clothing. Is that asking too much?" Greg pleaded piteously.

"You don't know the city, do you?" she said hesitantly.

"No, I don't. I need to find some place to stay. Please!"

"I can't help you, Armando," the girl whispered, brokenly. "It's between you and God. Now I know what you've done. It's evil, monstrous. Why? Why?"

"I wish I could explain it to you," he stammered badly. "It was because I…because I knew I could pull it off. This system—this government gets away with mass murder. It doesn't recognize a citizen like me. For all I've done, I got a kick in the ass. I became a government of one. People had to be punished."

Even through the silent line, he felt how horrified Lydia was, "I should've met you before, Lydia. I was…I was a solid chunk of ice. Now I realize, my heart is still beating…" The line was dead. Greg hung precariously over a chasm of despair, like his victims had hung on for dear life on the upper floors. Bloody pieces of humanity had spread across the street and splashed the buildings on the other side. Thinking of it now, it felt like someone was digging an iron fist in his stomach. It was nothing like what he had seen in the war. At the time he had done it, he thought to himself, *"It's cool, man, it's cool…"* Now he gagged as the bile rose to his throat.

Greg redialed. The telephone rang a couple of times, then he heard it being picked up only to be slammed down again. He was rejected even by a crazy girl.

Greg felt totally alone and isolated, a feeling very familiar to him. He had not admitted guilt, but nonetheless, guilt and emptiness permeated him. He hung up the phone and leaned in the corner of the booth, his chin and shoulders shaking with cold, unprotected from his previous bravado—he was feeling something akin to horror. *This* was a new feeling for him.

The rain was now coming down in sheets. Greg felt watched by the cashier. He gathered himself with a huge effort, moved like a sleepwalker to the ticket booth and bought a ticket. The middle-aged lady peered at him through the thick lenses of her eyeglasses.

"Are you OK?"

Greg tore his body from the support of the box office window, feigning indifference. "Yeah, I'm OK."

He walked to the restrooms and closed himself in one of the stalls.

"Now what?" he asked loudly. Suddenly, a tremendous burst of laughter came from the movie auditorium. He thought to himself—yeah, I'm a lot of laughs, folks.

Greg finally found a hotel and sat on the bed trying to think what to do next. Gregory wasn't big on thinking things through—he was someone who took action—sometimes rashly. He destroyed the identity of Armando Mejia and inspected the rest of Larry's forgeries. He decided on one, Red Grand. His new identity shared his reddish hair but sported a mustache. Fine with him. For appearance sake, it took a couple of patient days to get the mustache started, but it would suffice for now. The hotel bill and the purchase of some needed items of clothing nearly exhausted his funds. He did have enough left over to purchase a bus ticket to Montreal. It would be easier to disappear in a large metropolis.

From Hamilton to Montreal, Gregory MacPherson had a lot of time to kill. A seemingly endless ride through monotonous countryside. It lulled him back into a reoccurring dream he'd had since childhood. It obsessed him and grew in detail as it followed him into manhood. He had never felt that he belonged anywhere—always keeping to himself. The dream was an answer to his loneliness—he dreamed he was from another planet. It always ended the same way, with him jumping off into the void. But it was better than recalling how he had run away from home and missing high school graduation. He had escaped his abusive parents—the beatings—the drunken mess that had become a hell. "Shut up!" Greg hissed to himself.

One thing he never thought about was his past. He had forbidden himself to dwell on what was gone for good. So he stared emptily into space.

No! That wasn't true either! It had nothing to do with the real him! There was a stranger somewhere inside of him.

As he rode along in the bus, he tried to keep his mind empty.

Even when the weather changed from precipitation to sunshine, he rarely left the bus. A few passengers tried chatting with him. Understandably, he had avoided all conversation by feigning sleep, though he desperately kept awake. Sometimes, he talked in his sleep, and he certainly didn't want to say anything that would point a finger at Greg MacPherson.

Greg, as Red Grand, found a job as a sparring partner in a judo and boxing club. Officially he was a stand-in sparring partner, unofficially, *garcon pour tous;* in plain English, an errand boy. After closing time, he washed the mats, the floors, cleaned the showers, offices and dressing rooms. The manager paid him under the table below minimum wage. Some of the clients tipped him for small services, like bringing them coffee or sandwiches and giving them massages. He slept on the mats at night. It all suited him just fine for the moment. It kept him out of sight while he tried to think about his next move.

He was at the bottom of life, but then he had never known the heights. His scale of comparison was practically nil. Hookers appeased his sexual needs, free of charge, befriending him as one of their kind. Besides, he was a good lay.

A mobster discovered his abilities with firearms and took him to a local firing range. After studying his scores, he was impressed. When target practicing at the firing range, he easily beat the best shooters.

Red seemed strangely oblivious about life and death. He went down a notch by letting himself be contracted to murder for the Montreal mob. It was dangerous in the Montreal underworld, but Red Grand seemed fearless. The old head of the mobster association took a liking to Red, and he paid top dollar. Suddenly, Red Grand was feeling at the top of the world. Ups and downs in his life were almost a daily occurrence.

Greg MacPherson seldom thought about consequences, and as Red Grand, he hadn't changed a bit. His doubts in himself simply faded away.

The mobster boss took Red completely under his wing and Red soon became his personal bodyguard.

Red Grand rented a flashy, furnished apartment with access to large swimming pool and tennis courts. A car company—one controlled by the mob—gave him a special rate on a Ford *Mustang*. He was living like a millionaire, but kept on using loyal, cheap hookers. Why change what worked? Even at this point he didn't trust the old man.

In his mind, Lydia's presence always hovered in the background. Why? he asked himself. He didn't need her. Women were cheaper by the dozen. What would he say to her anyway?

As time went on, Greg's reoccurring dream, now encouraged by drugs, assaulted him with a vengeance. For quite a while, with his rich living, he had been successful in distancing himself from the dream's repetitive cycles. In his drug induced thoughts, he called them his *space diaries*.

In stark difference to Red Grand, Gregory MacPherson didn't feel any connection to the planet Earth. If Greg MacPherson was ever found dead, these strange, roughly scribbled writings would have been found on his body. And he meant for them to be.

DREAM DIARIES OF GREGORY MACPHERSON

I was born third generation on an interplanetary flight to our home planet Vegha 77.040009.

My dad was young, powerful and handsome. He laughingly called me Robinson Crusoe. He taught me how to move through the maze of our spaceship without a monitor. Mom wasn't as young or beautiful, but she helped me learn science and electronic deflagrations. I'm afraid most of that has been forgotten.

Mother was second-in-command. Her name was Clotilda Bauer, and she was addressed respectfully as Frau Professor. My dad, Archie, was just a part of the work crew. He played the accordion and was the life of each party and celebration.

Both of my parents expressed their love and pride in me (the best part of the dream). They gave me presents and boosted my confidence.

I called myself a child of love.

My dad took me to the gym as soon as I was steady on my feet. He was my trainer and taught me how to use all the gymnastic equipment. According to him, a man has to be brave and aggressive. He knew how to make the impression of being a tough guy and a prince charming as well.

Mother had little time for me except for my lessons. Her job on the ship was all consuming. However, she always came to my bed to kiss me and wish me good dreams. One of my mother's other children was Clara. She didn't like me. Sister Clara simply didn't like people. She said they bred like rats. I had never seen rats except on video.

Clara would purse her lips and say knowingly, "People have filled Earth to the brim. There is no room for us."

Then it dawned on me, that's the reason for traveling to a distant planet! It was people's fault! I started hating them, too.

For some unknown reason, my strange dreams always had the same ending: I was left behind on Vegha 77, intentionally or unintentionally. Left all alone in a bubble of enormous proportions, desperately trying to build a space-raft, like the very Robinson Crusoe my parents called me in fun. Then I would try to get back to the much hated (by me) planet Earth. I think, there were mental bridges that always fell to nothingness in the void. Then I would jump in total desperation from the rim of planet Vegha 77 and keep on falling forever.

The same ending—over and over.

Later, in Montreal, Greg made notes about his *Dream Diaries* in his sloppy handwriting, then sent them to Lydia. Gregory MacPherson roughly described his drug induced dreams to her and opened a P.O. box under an assumed name. After the fact, he became enraged with himself for sharing his most personal visions with someone he had met only once.

Greg checked the box every day.

There was no response from Lydia.

This made him even more angry with himself. He decided to write her off.

In Montreal, he failed to establish any meaningful relationships. He was never good at that, always feeling the odd man out. Now he was sure he came from the future. Most people around him spoke in French, which further alienated him. On his dream planet, Vegha 77, there were only imaginary visitors from other planets who spoke a strange gibberish. He planted a huge signpost that read, No Guests, Please!!!

Larry's younger brother was in Quebec but kept his distance from Greg. The Mafia in Canada wasn't as powerful as in the U.S. because of the French influence. The French had their own *Homme Dure* organization, mostly in renegade affairs. Snub-nosed as the French were, they wouldn't communicate with *garbage* like an *Americain* "wetback." Greg wrote them onto his shit-list where the greater part of humanity was already.

Italians had fewer scruples, and their natural flexibility served them (and him) well. So far Greg's whole life seemed imagined. He didn't care what was ahead of him. In his view, everything had already happened, especially with the help of drugs.

Larry's brother, angry at the fact that Greg had escaped and his brother had been caught instead, anonymously reported to someone he knew inside the mafia the true identity of Red Grand. After the mob *discovered* his past, Gregory MacPherson was put on an old freighter to the Middle East with a few dollars in his pocket. He was no longer eligible to be part of the mob, and they didn't want any attention from the law.

He was signed on to the cargo ship as a cabin boy. Actually, his job was the dishwasher. The mobsters wanted to humiliate him and they succeeded. He was told that he would be closely scrutinized if he took a plane. That didn't appease him. To make matters worse, he struggled against sea sickness almost the whole first week at sea. This was more proof in Greg's mind that he didn't belong anywhere—always the outcast. He had to escape—but where except more of Vegha 77.

Two

It was with great relief when he was able to be on dry land once more.

However, dry land didn't prove to be any better for him. Because Red Grand was a redheaded American, he wasn't embraced by the local Arabs in Beirut. He seemed headed toward more desolation, when, purely by chance, he met a certain Abdoulah Atta, a citizen of the world and free-thinker. Abdoulah, Abu to his friends, spent money like a Saudi prince, and seemed to be extremely influential on many levels. Abu even offered him a job as a paramilitary instructor of some Arabic groups in Afghanistan.

To Red, Abu appeared as a godsend, though what was *purely a chance* to Red wasn't chancy at all for Mr. Atta. He had read all the files on the young man previously sent by a "mole" in the mob. His *ideology* and character deficiencies, even his record while in the Marines were all there. There were two redeeming features in the eyes of Abu: this man hated his own country and wasn't squeamish about killing.

Though, a character like Gregory MacPherson wouldn't be able to understand martyrdom in a thousand years.

They sat in an open-air cafeteria at the seaside sipping ice-coffee. Abu Atta drew in the acrid smoke from his Turkish cigarette. "Americans would never accept your deep-seated idealism." This statement was said affably while he peered through his dark glasses at the somewhat rubicund face of Red Grand. "On them your altruism is wasted," he continued.

Red was taken by surprise. No one had ever described him like that, but it sounded true. Come to think of it, he wanted to make the world a better place. But, how could this man know about that?

Abu Atta grasped his hand. "I can read your soul, my brother. Allah has granted me this power. Together we can move mountains." It was getting hot and muggy, with no trace of a breeze, "Let's go for a swim, Red. We both need to cool off a bit."

They made their way down the steps, closely shadowed by Abu's Palestinian bodyguards. Beirut was brimming with different political fractions, still bearing the marks of a senseless fratricidal war.

The *brothers* stripped down to their swimming briefs, running into the tepid surf like two teenagers. For the first time since his "Big Bang," Red felt attached to life. They dove and swam, competing with one another in the waves. Red liked the challenge of another male. It made him feel twice the man he was to swim faster or dive deeper than his companion.

When they splashed out to the beach, Abu sent his guards to cool off in the water. He dried himself lightly, then passed the towel to Red. He pulled on his pants. Then, leaving his bodyguards behind—he beckoned to his *brother*. Red got dressed as well, then followed Abu to a

Mercedes convertible. They drove through downtown to a high-class bordello.

It was siesta time. Naked women's flesh softly gleamed in the darkened room; air-conditioning units purred like happy animals. Red hadn't seen anything like this in Montreal. Here, he had a zesty young woman for his complete enjoyment. Tingling, cool sprays of water pushed away the heat. Smoking a water pipe, a hot Jacuzzi bath and all the food one could eat while a gentle zither strummed discretely from a leafy background intensified the enjoyment. The new *brothers* exchanged partners, then Abu Atta asked for two more. It became a party—belly dancing, flutes, tambourines and drums, hot, spiced coffee, sweets and fruit, then an orgy of sex.

Red didn't believe in heaven or hell, but now he was experiencing what was to him a partial earthly paradise, though, for a person like him, nothing was totally satisfying.

Back in his hotel room, Red was seized by doubts. Not a thing in the universe was given away free. He threw off his shirt and pants, which were again soaked with perspiration, then he kicked off his sandals and threw himself in bed. The air-conditioning was erratic but working.

In spite of all the rhetoric and expenses lavished on him, he felt the phony clichés behind the words of his new brothel brother. Abu hasn't subdued an easy prey, he thought smugly to himself. The mind of this young American still resisted, filled with Gregory MacPherson's covenant and deeply rooted individual fanaticism. After all, Greg always acted on his own, an army of one. Emotionally Greg belonged only to himself.

Abu had mentioned something about sending him to Afghanistan of all places.

What was there for him in Afghanistan? From all that he had heard, Afghanistan could only be hell incarnate. But, could he say no? Unlikely. Abu wasn't kidding when he said, *"Traitors get their heads chopped off!"* He also said, "You must embrace Islam."

Red spoke to himself hush-hush, almost in a whisper. "Not that I care about religion, but Islam? What do I know about Islam? Zilch—nothing. Never read the Bible, now I'm supposed to read the Koran? Could I cheat Islam, as I cheated Christians? I doubt it, I seriously doubt it. They are in business like me, killing everyone. No consideration, no preferences. For all I know, I was safer in the U.S. At least Americans are predictable. Canada wasn't an option. Sadly, Vegha 77 is only available in my dreams. So, will Afghanistan be part of my skittish life? Even Abdoulah Atta is problematic. I really don't know him, but what's my choice? Surrender…or death? Living in a bubble, then the last jump." He shook his closely cropped head energetically, "No way, not yet."

Red bit his lip and looked around, wide-eyed. What if *they* are listening to him, taping him? Maybe they all could read minds; Abu certainly did.

He fell on the hard pillow with a moan. What's done is done. Israel would turn him over to the States. China was too far, he was damned everywhere.

And what if there *is* a God in Heaven?

The next morning the concierge called him to his desk. "Your spiritual adviser is here, Mr. Grand."

Red felt like his blood left him. "Where?"

"In the manager's office." The employee smiled conspiratorially, "Welcome on board, brother."

The young American stood for awhile, shackled by his indecision, then he stepped up to the manager's door and knocked lightly. The manager answered discretely as if he had been waiting by the door. "*Inshallah,*" he uttered as he let him in.

The mullah was young, perhaps Red's age. He extended his hands in a benediction. "All mighty Allah blessed you with wisdom, brother Red. Are you joining the flock of the right faith with your new name, Ibrahim Ghamal?"

So long, Red Grand!

Greg somehow liked the sound of the name Ibrahim Ghamal, and suddenly, Red felt blessed with indifference.

"Yes, I am joining the flock."

"Is Allah your only god?"

"He is."

"And by thy own will, your only holy book shall be the Koran?"

"It will."

"Mohammed is the prophet you recognize as the true prophet to the last day of your life?"

"He is."

"Turn this way, toward Mecca," ordered the mullah. "Fall down on your knees, put your hand over the holy Koran and swear in the great name of Allah and his only prophet Mohammed. Their enemies shall be your enemies."

Red followed the ritual, "I swear in the name of Allah and his prophet!"

The cleric smiled broadly. "Now there is nothing you should fear in this world but the rage of Allah. Blessed be the faithful! Let's go to the mosque."

Gregory MacPherson's army of one surrendered without a single shot fired. Red fell into the embrace of the mullah, then followed him with pretended meekness.

Inwardly, he was as empty as before. He had no idea what would happen to him in the holy shrine, though he was haunted by premonitions. He vaguely remembered Iraq, the battlefields of the Desert Storm, some of the naked cadavers. The heads of their penises were stripped of their protective hood. He couldn't stand the thought of that being done to him.

Holy mackerel! He remembered noticing during the sexual orgy that Abu Atta's prick had been cut. Why didn't he think about it? Well, if that's the price to stay alive. Abu had warned him, "heads off." It's only the head of his prick—just the outer layer of skin. It doesn't matter if it's done while still an infant, but at his age. Who would've thought of it. What do they use for this procedure, knife, clippers or some special instrument?

Oh, God, what a mess he had brought on to himself!

Would they stop the bleeding? Probably. In the meantime, who's gonna pee for him? The friendly mullah read his doubts.

"It's only a formality, brother Red," the young man droned reassuringly. "It doesn't hurt."

Like hell it doesn't, Red thought briskly. *It's not your prick. Yours had been done at birth, you don't remember anymore. What a bloody ritual!*

It was noontime and the streets were bustling with people, mostly men. The stores had piled their merchandise, food and fruit on the sidewalks. Red salivated as he consumed the smells. He had missed his breakfast and lunch. Would his host feed him after the ceremony? Red swore under his breath.

The mullah pretended not to hear but smiled sardonically. "What a beautiful day, Allah be blessed."

You won't sell that to me, holy bastard, Red thought angrily. *There must be vindication for me!* Then he said aloud, "Why do everything in one day, Hadje? Even the creation of this world took longer. Can we do it tomorrow and enjoy the beauty of this day?"

The young mullah shook his head, "No. Tomorrow you'll be scared even more."

"Me, scared?" Red snapped back. "Nothing scares me."

In his deep, velvety baritone, the mullah laughed vigorously. "Prove it, Brother. Prove it now."

Three

Red, traveling as Ibrahim Ghamal, was flown from Beirut to Damascus where he was introduced to some internal security officers and intelligence agents fluent in English. They seemed to know everything about his past, though no one was shocked or dwelt on it. The unanimous decision was that he should study the language and indoctrination in a provincial area outside the city. Damascus was closely scrutinized by foreign institutions and agencies. His presence had to be kept hidden.

Red, as Ibrahim, was taken for granted. No one sought his personal opinion and rightfully so. The dazed feeling he experienced qualified him more as an object than as a human being. In his hotel bed, he was unable to ponder the situation. He slept the sleep of the dead, waking up with no expectations or hopes. It's possible that his food had been drugged; he had no will of his own. Snippets of a bustling oriental city, as if seen on TV, passed before his glassy eyes.

He shook hands with men of different ages and stature, answered questions, then listened to Arabic gibberish.

He was in a man's world; not a single woman was presented to him.

He was taken to a gym. He stood in the middle of a blue mat, facing another man—an environment hazily familiar. The other man was his opponent. Red's fighting instincts were automatically activated.

He parried an attack and hit his protagonist in the throat using a saber-blow with the sharp edge of his hand. The man fell flat on his face, writhing in agony. A larger man came to the mat. Red disposed of him with a foot to the crotch. Someone came at him from behind. Now, Red became a fighting machine. He saw the stick falling toward him in his mind's eye, dodged aside, though it slashed across his face, Red caught the man's neck and thrust him down to the mat, pressing a knee to his windpipe. The eyes of his foe bulged out of their sockets, and his face turned crimson. Several pairs of hands tore him from his victim. He stood a little shakily on his feet, blood running from the gash on his face—no matter. Someone complimented him. He talked to another person dressed in a business suit. Red grasped a few English words.

"A beard would do the job. It's a waste to send him away. Abu Atta was right. His reflexes are superbly conditioned. He could learn on the job."

Ibrahim Ghamal was carefully weaned off drugs and promoted to *military trainer*. A personal translator and supervisor was assigned to him. They were inseparable, sharing the same room and shower in an unknown location. His name was Achram. Away from the mat, Lieutenant Achram taught Red Arabic using the holy Koran and by conversing.

The last Western veneer of the former American disappeared.

The man now called Ibrahim grew a short beard and his hair was professionally darkened. He didn't mind that, as long as brother Achram took care of his needs. Red didn't want to think beyond survival. Why should he? He was permitted to select women of his liking from a photograph album, meals were provided, as well as cigarettes or a water pipe now and then—Allah had pardoned all his sins, he had murdered only enemies, his mansion in *paradise— promised*. What else? At least for the moment, as Ibrahim, he had no dreams, no visions.

As an instructor, he held classes in the gym or outdoors. He was demanding and meticulous. His pupils had an inherent tendency for sloppiness, but if pressed hard, they were capable of acting with precision. Achram understood their problem, Ibrahim did not.

"My fellow countrymen are used to being under constant surveillance. If left on their own, they shirk their duties or pretend results. For most of them, corporal punishment is indispensable, for others, hate is inspirational."

Ibrahim was surprised. "Why hate?"

Achram's shifty eyes expressed hesitation, then he spoke a middle-eastern truism. "Hatred is a powerful fuel, brother. Greater than love."

Ibrahim was taken aback. "Is that in the Koran?"

"No, it isn't, but the mullahs can explain it," Achram told him, then he changed the subject.

Ibrahim sensed something fundamentally wrong. He didn't remember hate as a factor in anything he had heard in Christian teachings, but then he wasn't educated in spiritual areas. Achram's English was far from perfect. He might've bungled something. In the meantime, Red was picking up Arabic—at first just words and commands, then he started putting together sentences. The colloquial language still escaped him, but TV and movies helped. Reading was more complicated. It took systematic lessons, though a large number of his trainees had limited reading skills or none. Basically, not knowing how to read was protection against Ibrahim's tedious indoctrination, both political and religious. In the mosque, he did whatever everyone else did, apart from the mullah's preaching, he pondered over his personal problems.

Life in the Middle East didn't sit very well with Ibrahim. While going to school in America, he hadn't felt any deep cultural difference. Here, however, the class and gender separation baffled him. It smacked of medieval times. Especially functions and places forbidden for females. He learned to address a married woman only in the presence of her husband or an elderly chaperon. Even then the answer came in a roundabout way. Most of them hid their faces behind veils or *ferdegee.*

His stomach didn't agree with Middle Eastern cooking. He had to get used to it. His unhappiness wasn't a matter of different opinions—it was the way of life that rubbed Red wrong. His lack of background culture made him inflexible. His lack of understanding kept him constantly short tempered. The physical nature of his chores vented some of his frustration—he could take it out on his students. It also prevented his Muslim colleagues from noticing his persistent irritation. Corporal punishment was encouraged, a broken arm or leg was par for the course. His bosses thought highly of him, but no pay. Just food and lodging.

Most of all, Red didn't take his religious commitment seriously. That would surely backfire on him sooner or later. In a large, cosmopolitan city like Damascus, his behavior wasn't as obvious, as his transfer to Afghanistan was imminent.

Ibrahim Ghamal still didn't know that he was training terrorists, instead of a regular army. He didn't think of himself as a terrorist.

Before long, he and lieutenant Achram were on a nonstop flight to Tehran. Red's teacher and guide was in foul mood. He had been given no time off to say good-by to his family. Talkative by nature, he didn't say a word for the most of the flight. He pretended sleep, but his anger manifested itself in grinding his teeth and swearing under his breath, fists clenched in silent anger.

Red wasn't quite sure where Afghanistan was. He had forgotten to look at the map. As Ibrahim Ghamal he had no control over his life. Even survival didn't matter anymore.

The awesome enormity of what he had done in his native country gradually came into focus. Suddenly he was horrified with himself. He should've died in the blast. It was like coming out of a chrysalis state. Operation Desert Storm…the medal. He didn't know anyone in Waco. He remembered seeing Oklahoma shown repeatedly on television. He saw that Larry came on with a vague description of what had taken place. It was worth nothing. Larry told the police that Gregory MacPherson had had the experience. He had been in the Marines. Greg had made a visual recognizance of the building. He said it could work. He would use a huge load of explosives in midmorning!

Then, "BANG!" It became reality, as easy as that.

Maybe there is a God after all—and a hell. God is everywhere, even in Afghanistan. On that flight, Ibrahim was unable to sleep, or even pretend to, like his companion Achram.

For Lydia life wasn't easy either. TV, radio broadcasts and newspapers threw more gas on the fire. Everyday, there were new horrendous details and discoveries, but Gregory MacPherson wasn't apprehended. Appeals came from everywhere. Pastors made it their duty. Parishioners were to report even the smallest suspicions. Lydia stopped going to church. Ian, her father, didn't insist. He wasn't religious anyway.

Lydia hardly touched her food. She lost weight and was unable to sleep. The school superintendent asked Ian to take her to a psychiatrist. Ian feared the outcome. What if she talks?

Then the underground became involved, and his assigned advisor gave him the name of a specialist in the field, a sympathizer to their cause. Lydia underwent therapeutic sessions. She was suffering severe chronic depression.

However, what Lydia couldn't or wouldn't tell anyone was what was causing her condition. Unbeknownst to her father, she had received Greg's "Dream Diary." That and the strong resemblance of what she felt her brother would have looked like if he had lived, caused a whirlwind of feelings to conflict with what she had learned about Greg. What if no one had loved her brother and turned their backs on him when he was in need? She was, indeed, haunted by her personal troubling thoughts of guilt—she had done nothing to help Greg.

"Listen, Ian," Dr. Mellville advised, "Your daughter needs help. She is definitely holding something back. You have to sign authorization for her to undergo deep hypnotic treatment."

"My answer is no." Ian was adamant.

"Explain this to your advisor."

At least, Dr. Mellville proscribed pills and a certain amount of time away from school. Lydia played out her haunted emotions with her puppet theater but kept her dad out of it. When Ian saw what she was doing, he reported it to the doctor. Dr. Mellville wanted to personally explore that aspect of her character, so he asked Ian to secretly tape her.

Ian taped one of her stage improvisations, though it made him feel like *Polonius* of *Hamlet*, who spied on his daughter. He set up a tape recorder on voice-activation. Late that night he listened to the recording. To him it sounded profoundly mature—well beyond his intellect. The play involved a spaceship traveling to a distant planet. Her dad could see, even without the expertise, that Lydia was a born actress and gifted playwright, besides something troubling in her mind.

There was a second part in the show. Lydia was speaking *his* lines as well as her own.

It was shocking. To Ian's knowledge, she had previously never had imaginary companions. Ian Grey rewound the tape and listened again.

"Don't be shy, now, you are an actor, brother," Lydia's voice chided. "This is an easy part."

Then she spoke, imitating the male voice, "Are you serious?"

"Of course I'm serious. It's my play."

"Well, if you say so…" it was the male voice. "I never played with puppets, though I've been playing with death since I can remember. I guess I could be Armando's voice-over if you move the puppet. It will fill our time until your father comes home."

Lydia clapped her hands. "Well…that at least is settled. Let's get going, Greg. Watch your step, the bulb is out—father hasn't changed it yet—so we have to play in semi-darkness."

Ian heard some shuffling steps, then more of Lydia's voice. "This is pretty Jenna. She loves Armando, but doesn't admit it even to herself. This one is Armando, a handsome boy, don't you think? But he doesn't love anybody but himself."

Ian was seriously alarmed. Was it really Lydia imitating a male voice or was there someone there with her? This ran through Ian's mind as he heard, "If Armando is naughty, why don't you kill him, Lydia? Just twist his head off."

"Oh, no-o-ooo!" Lydia screamed with extreme vehemence. "Don't ever say that again. I love him!"

Ian erased the recording. For the first time since the death of his wife, he felt really worried about Lydia. What if she was more mentally sick than he was aware of.

Four

A cargo plane brought Ibrahim and Achram to Kabul. By then, the lukewarm friendship between them had turned to hostility. Achram blamed him for being separated from his family, perhaps forever. Ibrahim thought of the young officer as his jailer. There was nothing to talk about. Both of them were thirsty and irritated. The plane landed at the airport under a blazing, hostile sun at two in the afternoon. The area looked dusty and deadbeat as the aircraft taxied lazily to a storage structure. When they got out, the tarmac had melted into gooey mush. It stuck to their boots and stunk of tar and shit.

The terminal was empty, save for a patrol in raggedy uniforms. Several pairs of dark, suspicious eyes, looked at the newcomers with a mixture of disdain and boredom. Flying, gritty particles invaded mouths and nostrils. The patrol's leader pulled down his shawl so he could talk.

"Are you the Syrians?" he growled.

Achram nodded and offered their papers. The leader pushed them aside and pointed at a large sign, *WELCOME TO THE FREE TALIBAN REPUBLIC!* That much even Ibrahim was able to read. He wished to be free of the tiny gnats and flies that came in swarms, but that was just an insignificant portion of the discomfort here. The locals didn't seemed bothered even by the lack of drinking water. Ibrahim and Achram tied their handkerchiefs midway across their faces. The Russian-made imitation of a WWII American Jeep took them over a bumpy road to downtown Kabul.

The city, if that name applied to the capital of Afghanistan, had been bombed innumerable times, then neglected. Parts of it seemed habitable, but not the center of town. Only portions of buildings stood in sharp contrast to their surroundings.

Achram whispered in Red's ear, "I wish I had never met you!" But, somehow, that sounded brotherly. Here, they felt alone, and instinctively stuck to each other like Siamese twins. At this time of the day, Kabul looked like a Hollywood backdrop for the city of the dead. The two *brothers*-in-misery were dropped off at one of the partially-restored buildings. It wasn't clear if it was a hotel or headquarters of some kind. At least they were served some chilled green tea with stale hard biscuits of unknown origin. The lobby, if it was a lobby, boasted three ceiling fans, of which only two moved. The receptionist told them to wait until four or five until someone was supposed to meet them. He invited them to use certain seating arrangements alongside the walls. A number of stinky bodies already slept there. The Syrian *brothers* were frisked for personal arms, then released to sit down.

Achram was too distraught to talk, but forced a few words in Ibrahim's ear. "This is the best part of our adventure, *American brother*. Prepare for the worst."

Ibrahim didn't have to prepare. He had resigned himself to his fate. He had earned every bit of it. In a way he felt for Achram. "Pray to Allah, if you can," he suggested to Achram.

The young Syrian was bitter. "Why, in Allah's name, did I have to learn English, of all languages?"

The American opened a new package of Egyptian cigarettes. They smoked in silence for awhile, then Achram lowered his boyish voice down to a whisper. "Do you know who Osama Bin Laden is?"

Ibrahim blew a stream of smoke through his nose. "Never heard of him. Am I supposed to know him?"

Achram shook his head. "Now you'll get to know him."

"Are we waiting for him?"

"Lower your voice, dummy," Achram ordered. "We won't see him now, but eventually we'll meet him. He is curious to see you. Birds of a feather, savvy?"

Ibrahim stared emptily at the cockroaches in the floor's crevices. "He must be evil incarnate," he muttered.

"Talking about yourself?" Achram suggested.

"In a way…" Ibrahim mumbled. "You read the papers about Greg MacPherson, didn't you?"

"Yes, after I was assigned to you. Why did you do what you did?"

Greg looked lost and confused. "Damn if I know! At the time, I thought I knew…"

"Lower your voice," Achram insisted, "the Taliban Republic is all about secret reports and listening devices."

A little after five-thirty, a black-bearded, turbaned man passed ceremoniously through the hall, greeted surreptitiously by the receptionist and the sleepers, all up and about. He seemed to be the head man of the place. Two guards followed him into his office, then one of them came back and spoke to the receptionist while looking at Lieutenant Achram and his charge.

"Are you the foreigners?" he asked formally. Achram presented their credentials. The guard took them without a glance, obviously illiterate. "Mullah Habbib will see you now. Follow me."

He placed the credentials in front of the black-bearded man, then retreated to the door. The mullah had a fat face and piggy eyes lost in bags of flesh. He adjusted the steel rimmed eyeglasses on the bridge of his nose, reading here and there, then peered at the young men.

"Which one of you is the American?" This was asked in a surprisingly high pitched voice. Red stepped forward, "Ibrahim Ghamal, also known as Gregory MacPherson, now of the Muslim faith," Ibrahim nodded curtly.

"Your deed has impressed a great friend of ours." The mullah went on, "Are you ready to meet him?"

Greg/Ibrahim had nothing else to do.

Five

From Kabul Lieutenant Achram and Ibrahim Ghamal were driven to Herat.

The countryside was mostly desert with a few miserable cultivation experiments. The villages were beyond description, no changes for the last ten thousand years. The inhabitants knew about radio, television and moving pictures but didn't trust them, and rightfully so. They did receive broadcasts that were 100 percent vicious, *religious*, anti-Western propaganda. Pestilence had spread everywhere, and there was no medical help whatsoever. It was Allah's will. A few foreign missionaries fought an ever-losing battle. The heat, minus regular input of liquids and nutrients, leads to the disintegration of body and brain faculties.

Herat had suffered fewer bombings, but was less urbanely organized compared to Kabul. There were a few mosques and palaces that stood in sharp contrast to Herat's narrow alleys and clay-stucco housing. Earthquakes, abundant on the great Euro-Asian fault, had had devastating effects.

The ancient Russian *Volga*, crossed the city, right through its bumbling market filled with contraband goods and hard drugs.

The Russian car, leaving its heavy exhaust of smog behind, continued further south. No one revealed to the foreign guests their final destination, and they had learned not to ask questions. Under Taliban rule, silence was a virtue.

Finally, after changing two flat tires, the *guests* and their guards reached a building, supposedly the Afghanistan equivalent of a European castle, minus any architectural value. The whole crew was dusty, dead tired, thirsty and hungry. Food wasn't offered, just small cups of tepid tea.

Waiting for big shots in a middle-eastern country is part of the venue. The higher the rank, the longer the wait. Sometimes one had to come again the next day or a third. Even then, one might never get the chance to meet the exalted person.

Amazingly, Ibrahim Ghamal was ushered in shortly after his arrival, but Achram the guide was stopped at the door.

"The American only," the usher stated unequivocally.

Ibrahim was lead in front of two elderly, bearded and turbaned men, seated cross-legged in middle-eastern fashion. One was gaunt in face and body, the other plump and shorter.

"Welcome, Mr. Gregory," the lanky man said with a Mona Lisa smile, "My name is Osama, and this is my partner." Bin Laden's English was good, almost fluent, "Sit down and help yourself."

There was a variety of fruit, sweets, teacups and tea laid out in front of the hosts. The *guest* sat down, in the same manner as his hosts, and peeled a banana. "Thank you, sir." He ate it in two bites, then helped himself to some grapes.

His host went on, ignoring the famished eating of the American. "I have to admit that Omar and I were pleasantly surprised to discover an un-American American. I know what I'm talking about, I've been to the States. Frankly, I discredited Mr. Atta. Then I read about you. You participated in the Iraqi war you called Desert Storm, and distinguished yourself. Am I wrong, Mr. Gregory?"

Ibrahim swallowed a few grapes. It was nice to hear his real name from someone else.

"So far, you are right, Mr. Osama."

Then the older man said almost gently, "Your heroic deed—did you do it on your own?"

Greg was blunt, "An associate helped me put together the explosives. But the rest was all my doing." Greg was somehow shocked to hear himself speaking in English.

Osama laid a bony hand on Omar's shoulder and smiled broadly.

"Allah be praised! The children of the world are our insurance policy for the future. We are not alone." He turned again to Greg, "You became a Muslim and changed your name of your free will?"

"I think so," Greg hesitated.

"So now, you are Ibrahim Ghamal?" Osama asked plainly.

"I am," Ibrahim whispered.

"Did you hear that, Omar?" Osama exclaimed. "This world is so politically polarized, it's ripe for falling into our hands. Western European powers are so afraid of us that they would compromise to appease us. Our demands certainly won't come to an end before we destroy their perverted civilization. The Germans eat shit out of our hands, the Russians are meek and lazy, miring themselves in endless negotiations, France is our spittoon, Spain is falling apart, and the almighty U.S. faces civil war, degeneration and economic disaster. Allah is unleashing punishment after punishment upon them. Didn't I tell you so? Our priority is to attack their Sodom and Gomorrah— Hollywood and Las Vegas."

"No, my friend," Omar mused. "Money comes first. Sooner or later, we will have to start attacking schools and hospitals. Westerners cannot stomach that. Traffic and transportation must be brought to a standstill. So, I ask, how can you be so sure that this young man is not a CIA mole or an agent of international Zionism?"

Osama wasn't amused by these unfounded accusations. "I believe in Atta as I trust my own soul. Ibrahim Ghamal has never been to Israel, never known a Jew. He is the Islamic transfiguration of the heroic Gregory MacPherson. He killed infants in a daycare center without batting an eye. Let's ask him." Turning his attention back to Ibrahim, he asked, "Where do you think we should hit now, Ibrahim?"

Ibrahim thought shortly then answered, as if an automaton, "The World Trade Center."

Omar felt suspicious, "Ha! Atta told you."

Ibrahim shook his head, "He told me nothing."

"We tried the towers already, in 1993," Omar hissed.

"Ramzi Yousef didn't do it right, Your Holiness. The amount of explosives was ridiculously inadequate. The specific power of the chosen explosive should be distributed in accordance with every cubic foot of the interior, then placed in the middle of the building," Ibrahim advised brazenly.

Omar bristled, "This man is dangerous, Osama. Don't trust him."

Osama Bin Laden brought his eyebrows together, throwing a thunderous look at his closest friend. "I don't trust anyone, Omar, including you. But Abu Atta has a special place in my soul. Didn't you just hear me say so? How many times do I have to repeat it? This youngster across from us is going nowhere, though we will use his knowledge for the good of our cause. If you know what's good for you, don't teach me how to live, Omar. The World Trade Center was bungled, and your blind colleague that was in charge was truly blind. From now on, Allah be blessed, I'm going to use only young fanatics, and that's my will! Get out, Omar, and don't pick up an extension. I'm watching the control panel."

Omar left, but not before throwing Greg MacPherson, aka Ibrahim Ghamal, a poisonous glance. Osama moved the pillow closer to him, then invited his young guest, "Come sit next to me, Ibrahim, so we can talk quietly."

Ibrahim sat cross-legged on the right side of the gaunt but *gentle-faced* person. He felt the spiritual attraction of the prematurely-aged man, mixed with the merciless hypnotic power of a cobra.

"Listen to me, Ibrahim," he murmured. "At the site of your deed you had people of all walks of life, young and old, some toddlers as well. What did you feel before activating the explosives?"

Ibrahim had no secrets, at least for the time being.

"As I was attacking the enemy, I felt nothing, Babba."

Osama clapped his large, skeletal hands. "Allah be blessed! He has given you the spirit of a great Islamic warrior." He almost touched Red's knee, but stopped at the last moment, "Now, tell me, what you felt in the aftermath, my son."

The young man didn't delay his answer even for a fraction of a moment. "Solitude…and total isolation, more than I had ever felt before."

Osama's hand moved away from his knee jerkily, as if he had been dangerously close to touching a hot plate. "What about now, under the generous protection of Allah?"

Ibrahim openly met the cold stare of his host. "I don't know yet, Babba."

Osama Bin Laden dismissed him laconically with a motion of his lanky hand. "Let me know when you have a ready answer, Ibrahim."

Achram was nowhere in sight. Red asked about him. His new *brothers* laughed, *such a man never existed!* Red got the message. He could trust no one, and no one would trust him. A traitor of his kind is not to be trusted by anyone!

His Arabic fluency was still in the fledgling stage, and the commandos surrounding him didn't speak English. Out of the training facility, he was condemned to solitude. In a week's time he was flown to an outpost near the Pakistan border. It could've been Vegha 77 minus the protective bubble. Dust and desolate rocks to the very end of the horizon. Headquarters was housed in intricate caves. With air so stale, it was hard to breath.

A new translator was assigned to him. Red, as Ibrahim Ghamal, taught the making of explosives and martial arts. The mountain people were hostile yet introverted. Red didn't try to make any friends. His days were monotonous, his nights lonely. Meals were unsatisfying and far apart. Even in his worst nightmares he hadn't expected this.

The solitude in these mountains was frightful—no trees, no grass, no birds—especially during the nights when the prolonged howls of unknown wild animals and the sudden gusts of wind swept over the barren landscape. There wasn't a communal shower. A rub down with snow, if available, had to do the job. Everyone smelled of rot and was covered in layers of dirt that looked like skin-scabs, so it didn't matter.

Six

gent Cliff was listening to a briefing for employees at his level on the latest in terrorism. It was practically regurgitating former attacks, schemes and leads. The newest was classified above his grade, but some rumors had reached him. Besides the blasts in Africa, there were new terrorist cells throughout the USA, absorbing a wave of dangerous elements coming in from Mexico and Canada. Some were closely watched, others were undetectable. No arrests were made so as not to compromise the sources of information. President Clinton didn't believe an imminent attack was in the making. The French and the German Intelligence had assured him there wasn't. However, he did advise extreme caution. After the bombing of al-Qaeda centers in Afghanistan, the enemies were busy reorganizing. No panic, time works in our favor.

Clinton was coming to the end of his second term. He didn't want complications with the Allies.

Cliff left disgusted. His gut feeling was telling him that something was on the fire. What would the reaction of the newly-elected president be? Will he close his eyes to the obvious? The CIA and the FBI were badly affected by the radicals in the Government. Their staff cut, their prerogatives not appreciated. Many agents were discouraged and disappointed. The morale after Jimmy Carter's fiasco as President was low. Reagan tried restructuring the agencies when he came into office but couldn't finish the job. Clinton tried also but not fast enough. Everyone was overworked. Army Intelligence wasn't trusted. There was practically no link or communication between all the different agencies.

Cliff drove his car toward his home in Falls Church. Should he resign from the CIA? His family was falling apart. He was always absent. Lora thought he had lovers. His young daughter hardly knew him.

He sacrificed them both, and for what? For the safety of his country? No way. Safety in the U.S. was virtually nil, only complacency. He felt uneasy about facing Lora. What else could he do for a living? His pension would be insufficient to live off of.

Cliff hit the steering wheel. "Damn! Damn! Damn!" There must be an honorable exit for his twenty years on the service. He wasn't a quitter. He had a lead on a professor in a Florida university. Who would believe someone like Agent Cliff? The professor was thought of very highly by the radical left and no viable proof was against him as yet. To penetrate such a solid Alma Mater was next to impossible.

He thought of himself as an army of one.

Ibrahim, as Greg, sank into a deep depression that evolved into indifference. In the depths of his spiritual and physical isolation, out of nowhere, he remembered the teenage girl from Hamilton, Canada. Her phone number was still in his wallet.

To call Lydia at any price, became an obsession. But how? And when? The time difference was great. How great? Between fourteen and sixteen hours. Who, then, was to be approached? The switchboard operator at the bunker or Ibrahim's immediate commander—perhaps both? If he called at nine in the evening local time, it would be t. ree in the afternoon in Hamilton. It gradually grew to be a ı atter of life and death to him. He kept postponir , and postponing, until one evening he decided ´   ´

He caught himself praying, to God oı .ьıah.. ᵈid it matter? *"Oh, God, whoever you are, for the first and last tiмıe I pray to You! Let it be "yes," or I don't know what to do with my life…"*

The commander and an aide were in the switchboard operator's room. Greg approached the door, licked his parched lips, found his rocky voice and pleaded.

"Brother Commander?" He swallowed nervously, "Can I…can I, please make a telephone call?"

The commander didn't even turn to see him. "Of course not!" he snapped rudely. Then a vaguely familiar voice intervened, "Where to, Ibrahim? The U.S.?"

It was Abu Atta!

Greg stepped backward with surprise. "Hamilton, Canada," he whispered, shaking with surprise and fear.

Abu looked at him carefully. He realized the enormous physical and moral change in his former American *brother*. He was like the ghost of the young man he had known. Ibrahim's experience in this cold mountainous outback, plus his use of drugs to maintain some sort of sanity, had deeply augmented his appearance. His scar from his injury was more pronounced than ever. Abu nodded, "Canada is okay, *brother*. Come in."

The commander felt he had been overridden, so shrugged his shoulders and repeated mechanically, "Come in."

Greg entered the room like an unwanted, mangy cur and handed the piece of paper to the operator. The al-Qaeda operator glanced at it and looked at Abu Atta. Abu approved it.

The operator invited Greg to sit on his bench, then looked at the codes glued to the key pad. "The link may not be clear, *brother*," he said in halting English.

"I know," Greg nodded, trying to get his nervous shudder under control.

"Do you want me to make it, person-to-person?"

"Yes, please," Greg said hesitantly.

The operator dialed a score of numbers, then handed the receiver to Greg. The line crackled several times. The chances of finding Lydia at home were slim. She must have graduated from high school by now and was either working as someone's secretary or adjusting to college if she hadn't completely succumbed to madness. The line was overcome by heavy static. Drops of sweat ran down Greg's smudged face. Suddenly the telephone line became clear, and the ringing was loud and distinct. On the forth ring the receiver was picked up.

It was Lydia!!!

"Hello…hello…"

Greg had a problem finding his voice.

"Talk!" The operator urged.

Greg felt as if he was shouting, but actually he was whispering. "Lydia…Lydia, please don't hang up…"

Even after a two-year time lapse, she recognized Armando's voice but now knew his real name. At first, she was unable to utter a word. Then she mastered some kind of coherence. "Is that really you, Greg? Where are you?"

Greg licked his lips again, "I don't know exactly. Somewhere in Asia."

There was a terrible pause, in which he thought the connection was lost, but Lydia's voice came through. "Armando and Jenna were asking about you. They think you are a captive, but not on Vegha 77. Your partner Larry got several life sentences. Capital punishment is still possible on federal charges. On TV, he looks pitiful. Was he for real? His brother is still in Canada, trying to muster support…"

"Larry deserves death," Greg mused. "So do I. You are always in my thoughts."

There was a longer pause, yet the line was amazingly clear. The operator turned to Abu Atta. "If we stay on the air for more then two minutes, we could be detected."

"Stay!" Abu ordered dryly.

The line came to life, bringing Lydia's voice. "I think of you often too, Greg. Why, in the name of God, did you do it?"

"I wish I knew, Lydia, but I hope to see you once again…"

The line crackled and died. Greg handed the receiver back to the operator, then ran out of the room, Abu ran at his heels. Greg thrust himself in a corner of the dark hallway, hands covering his face, shoulders shuddering compulsively. Abu Atta put his hands on his back.

"I know what you feel, if what I think matters to you."

Greg turned his ravaged face streaked with angry tears. "Do you?" He said harshly, "Then, explain it to me."

"There is little to explain, Ibrahim," Abu said with a degree of kindness. "I have a girl that I love, but I'll die as a martyr."

Greg smiled forlornly.

"If that's the case, *brother*, you don't give a damn about her."

Abu shook his head. "You don't understand, Ibrahim. I'll die for her, so she can live in a new and righteous world."

"How can you be so cocksure what's right and what's wrong?" hissed the American.

Abu Atta offered him a cigarette, then lit it and his own, trying to cover up his disappointment. "You are still an atheist, are you not?"

Greg pondered this, then came up with something like a grunt, or it might've been a sigh. "Not anymore, Abu. I don't understand Allah's will, but to me His existence is a proven fact. What I don't believe in is coincidence. All events are preordained, aren't they?"

Abu Atta leaned on the coarse, peeling wall next to him. "Of course, and some of them have happened already. We call it, *THE WILL OF ALLAH*. You can still join the club, if you want."

Greg looked at him mistrustfully. "What's in it for me, if I join?"

"Your destiny," Abu declared with conviction. They smoked in silence listening to the howling of the wind, then Abu Atta started again, "I am taking a flight from Pakistan to Baghdad, then to Prague and from there to Canada. Are you interested?"

Greg was stunned. "Are you kidding me?"

"Not at all?" Atta shrugged his shoulders. "Osama likes you. Are you afraid?"

"What could be more frightful than being alive in suspended animation?"

Abu boxed his shoulder. "You are incorrigible. I won't mention that part of our conversation to Bin Laden. He thinks of you as an American hero, though he doesn't trust you. I'll try to change your mind if you are willing to cooperate."

Greg's cigarette hung from his lips. "I'll try anything, just get me out of this inferno, please. I'm ready to splash my brains on this wall."

"That would be a waste," Abu puffed at his cigarette. "When you do it for an elevated cause you can go directly to Heaven."

"Your cause?" Greg asked.

"Our cause," Atta corrected him.

Seven

A thirty-two year-old heals fast.

Just a few days in Karachi made Greg feel like a different man. Lying by the ocean or the hotel swimming pool, regular meals in first class restaurants and walks on busy, commercial streets got him back in shape. Night time, appropriately dressed, he visited the luxury bars and night spots accompanied by *free lance* girls. This quickly restored Greg's self esteem and arrogance. He didn't forget about Lydia, yet he didn't think about her, either. Even with a telephone in his hotel room, he made no effort to call Hamilton again.

Abu Atta paid the bills, but seldom was with him as he had plenty of *business meetings*. All Greg had to do was ask and he got what he wanted, be it drugs, booze or women.

Their flight from Karachi to Sadam Airport in Baghdad was uneventful. A new, chauffeur-driven *Mercedes* was waiting for them. It didn't take them to a hotel but straight to the private residence of *Prince* Udde, son of the omnipotent dictator of Iraq. Udde's residence was built on the grounds of his father's most extravagant palace. Greg felt a bit uncomfortable, but his jovial host assured him that baba Hus'ney loved Americans. Udde went out of his way to show Greg the town, especially the nightlife. Abu Atta had his own business schedule, mostly under the patronage of Sadam's other son, who Greg never met.

In a private session with his American guest, Udde got drunk as a sailor.

"I love Americans…" He kept on repeating, "I love Americans like you, brother. You did what you did to avenge us, didn't you?"

He showed him his collection of sex-albums, which he called the *extraordinary art of masochism*. Greg didn't know the meaning of the word *masochism*, but after seeing those albums he learned fast.

"We are all martyrs, Ibrahim, you kn-no-w th-that…" He stuttered, stroking his well-trimmed moustache.

All Greg felt was a deepening nausea. Udde wasn't joking; he took himself seriously. Greg decided to take advantage of his intoxication.

"Is al-Qaeda a business or a political organization, Mr. Udde?" He pretended naiveté.

Suddenly Udde's eyes turned opaque. "I don't know what are you talking about," he mumbled. "Abu Atta is just a buddy of my brother's. They may have some business ties. However, none of us is involved in politics."

That was a blatant lie. Ibrahim Ghamal was probably considered fictitious as well. He finished his drink.

"You never heard of al-Qaeda, Mr. Udde?" Greg's inquiry might've signed his death sentence.

Udde's eyes turned cold. "This so called organization is just a figment of the CIA's overactive imagination. Iraq is a peaceful, nonaligned country."

Abu Atta had disappeared. One of the guards gave Red a short typewritten note, no date, no signature.

Mission changed, going to Africa. You haven't been seen in a mosque. Join the prayers, Allah is great!

Greg couldn't believe this was happening. He was sent like a package on a transportation flight to Kabul, then loaded on a military convoy that traveled to the Chechen border. Another stronghold in the rocks, the same routine—explosives and martial arts. This time he felt he had to join in the communal prayers, at least symbolically.

No spiritual feed back. There were rumors about more heroic actions in Africa and reports of American retaliations in the south.

Death to America!

Agent Cliff received a small package from a friend of his on the Canadian Mounted Police Force. A box of French bon-bons. At the bottom of the box was an updated, coded list of communist participants connected to the underground.

Somehow, Cliff's eyes fell on the name Ian, then added in his own hand, "daughter, possibly linked to Gregory." Cliff remembered MacPherson had escaped via Canada. In a computer file, Cliff found more about Ian's daughter. She was an ardent, radical activist at the university and had a background of mental collapses.

Cliff made a mental note to follow up on this information.

The winter came early, harsh and unforgiving. Bare, desultory mountains and total isolation reigned. No baths and no running water. Days and nights ran together without meaning. Greg lost track of time. Fighting the lice infestation was fruitless because lice were everywhere. Local people never heard of DDT. Consuming drugs was the only relief from the constant itching.

During one of the recreation periods in the training, Greg sat against the wall next to a guy as dirty and raggedy as he was, though not a Chechen and certainly not an Afghan. Was he Russian? Without looking at him Greg whispered, "Russkey?"

"No. I'm like you," the other answered quietly. "A rebel without a cause."

"Are you?" Greg glanced at the guy while scratching his head. "No one is like me." It was a pleasure speaking English instead of stumbling in Arabic.

"I know who you really are, Ibrahim—you are a legend," the other mumbled reverently.

"Spare me," Greg retorted. "*Nightmare* is the right word to describe me and my deed. A never ending nightmare. What's your name?"

"Jonathan Mahdy."

"Are there other Americans, Mahdy?"

"Call me Joe if you please. I'm pissed with the *Mahdy*. Can't stand it." Then Joe answered his question, "There are two girls, missionaries from the States, down in Kabul," he announced confidentially. "Got any smokes?"

"None," Greg swore under his breath, "just the fucking hash."

"What's gonna happen to us, coach?"

Greg shrugged his shoulders. "More of the same, I guess."

The rest period was over. Who was this Jonathan? Could he be a decoy? Greg engaged him in the introduction of new holds. Up close, Greg could tell that Joe's hair had undoubtedly been darkened. The youth didn't smell like a traitor. What does a traitor smell like? Probably like the greatest stinker of them all, Gregory MacPherson! Greg giggled.

"What ya laughing at?" Joe whispered.

"At myself," Greg whispered back and threw him on the floor roughly, announcing loudly in Arabic, "Death to America!"

At least, now, there were two American sons-of-bitches in the same hellhole.

Eight

The two *compatriots* were careful not to be seen together, except on active duty. Then they talked Arabic. Jonathan had gone through two schools in Saudis Arabia and Pakistan, so his Arabic was better than Greg's, but the local dialect was difficult for both of them. Joe walked into this mess on his own. His parents were well-paid government employees, though by conviction, extreme liberals. Joe's brother and two sisters had become moderately indoctrinated. Unfortunately, Joe was a mama's boy, and his mother hated the American *imperialistic capitalism* passionately. She thought social revolution imminent. Joe became a *hater* to please his mom; otherwise he wasn't a fighter.

Handsome was the right word to describe him. He had broad shoulders, a massive chest and thighs, biceps a hundred percent muscle. His face was on the rugged side, but with large brown eyes guarded by long lashes, and his lips were masculine but sensual.

Joe had heard many tales about Waco's battle and the blasphemous deed done by Gregory MacPherson. His parents stoked the fire by participating in candlelight vigils. Joe was indoctrinated to the gills with propaganda against the U.S. He participated in protest meetings and rallies, then eventually, he ran away to the Near East. He had little problem recognizing Greg even though Greg was disguised. Greg had become his role model.

"Now, you're getting more than enough of my stink," Greg stated flatly.

The two *anonymous* chums found an isolated niche for their bedding, so they were able to exchange whispers in the freezing winter nights. They had no furloughs to the village, but even if they had, their chances of any liaisons were zilch. Young females were kept under constant surveillance. Alcohol was forbidden. The males in the rambling stockade had to either go without or improvise sexual relief on their own. The mullah didn't mind interaction as long as the flock joined prayers.

"Have you met the *great man*, Joe?" Greg asked.

"In Peshawar," Joe confided, "The old goat, purred like a tomcat, *Mahdy, you'll become a great warrior!* Big warrior my prick. Then I was still a fuddy-duddy." Joe spat aside and helped himself to some hash, "I wonder what *they* plan to do to the *Great Satan*?"

They could only speculate.

The night was bitterly cold. As a matter of survival they pressed against each other tightly. Joe was silent for awhile, then mumbled in Greg's ear, "Are you going to shoot at your fellow Americans?"

Greg groaned, "I murdered quite a few already." A sizable nervous tremor shook Joe's body. "Be grateful, Joe, that you haven't killed anyone yet. Gregory MacPherson is a mass murderer." The youth wriggled, obviously uncomfortable. "Hiding behind a Muslim name doesn't help a bit," Greg admitted. "I have to live with my crime for the rest of my life.

"You belong to a loving family that will stand by you to the last. I don't expect friendship from you. No commitments on either side. I'm just being practical—helping each other like any bastards would do, back to back against a common enemy. I am not on the lookout for excuses or understanding."

"For the hell of it, whoever you are, please love me!" Joe begged.

Greg's body became limp, almost lifeless, his heartbeat hardly felt. "I can't, Joe. I cannot love anyone. No man and no woman. Hear me. **No one!!!**"

He was lying. He still dreamed about Lydia every night. He imagined making love to her.

The awakening was rude and painful. He was the same old jerk.

Ibrahim Ghamal volunteered to fight in a Chechen unit, just to get away from Joe. On active duty there was a possibility of being killed, but that seemed better than to go on living where he was. Chechens were known to be fearless and their cruelty went beyond normal standards. Torture and the decapitation of prisoners, traitors and collaborators were to be expected. Joe stayed back, he lacked real fighting courage, though he still nourished some kind of blind hope. For an American of twenty-one, miracles were still possible.

Expectation of survival was practically nonexistent. **Al-Qaeda** built its martyrs' cells on the principal—*die for a better life.* Palestinians found themselves in the identical, desperate straits.

While waiting for his transfer, Greg avoided being around *brother* Mahdy. Since Joe was afraid of Greg's daredevil resoluteness, he stayed out of Greg's way. The mama's boy's pathetic emotions were appeased solely upon his daily use of hash. He didn't know any more about love than Greg did.

Greg disliked the pampered boy intensely. For an inexplicable reason, to him, Joe's good looks were repulsive. Lydia was unattainable, except in his dreams. What else was there besides hash and self-relief?

However, the transfer from headquarters didn't materialize. Instead, a messenger from the local chieftain told Ibrahim Ghamal he had an important message waiting for him.

What could be wrong? Greg pondered while walking with the liaison, *And why meet in the chieftain's private residence, instead of at the stockade?*

The answer was very simple. High Command had sent a confidential fax.

To Ibrahim Ghamal. Come to Herat without delay. Transportation provided.
A.A.

That had to be Abu Atta. A helicopter waited for Greg. The chieftain said everything was arranged. He didn't have to report to the fort. Actually, he was ordered not to say "good-by" to anyone. Not a word!

The helicopter took him to the nearest air base, where an ancient MIG jet stood ready to leave. It took off as soon as Greg was designated the gunner's seat. The noise and the vibration was so disturbing that Greg was unable to think. The magnificent sights of the Hindu Kush Mountains escaped him, his goggles fogged by his exhaled breath. On arrival he had hard time pulling himself together. He was helped out of the jet and eased down the ladder like an old man.

In the same lobby as his first arrival in Afghanistan, Greg was given a cup of coffee and a bite of overcooked meat. He remembered the young Syrian who had previously accompanied him. Only Allah knew what had happened to Lieutenant Achram.

It was past noon but not as stiflingly hot as before. On one of the hard, wooden benches, Greg fell into an exhausted sleep. He slowly came awake when he felt someone shaking his shoulder.

It was Abu Atta. He sat next to him and offered him a cigarette. They smoked silently, then Abu said tersely, "This time you are coming with me."

Ibrahim Ghamal exhaled the tart smoke. "Am I entitled to know where?"

"I thought you'd remember," Abu smiled patronizingly.

"Prague and Canada?"

"You might be able to see Lydia," Atta stated matter-of-factly.

Greg's face remained expressionless. But inside, his stomach seemed to do flip-flops. For the first time, against all odds, he would see Lydia again. "Do you really believe in Allah, Abu?" Greg quizzed.

Atta nodded his head nervously, "Of course, I do!"

"Then, how can you be whatever you are?" Greg uttered calmly.

"I serve Him, don't you?" Abu bounced back.

"I don't know, brother Abu. God never asked me for anything."

"Didn't you have some offerings, brother Ibrahim?"

Greg lifted his eyebrows, "I doubt if any of my offerings were ever accepted in Heaven."

"But you did what you did anyway, didn't you?" Abu's sarcasm reverberated through Greg's mind and heart.

"I did it for the hell of it and got it flush back in my face," he retorted. "I should've been a martyr to my cause, then I would've been accepted in Paradise, am I right?"

Abu Atta placed his hand on Greg's shoulder, peering into his eyes. "Dead right."

They boarded a flight to Tehran.

Nine

During the flight they were both tense and jittery—no conversing or napping. Greg didn't trust Atta any more than Abu trusted him. But the mastermind terrorist thought that he held the American in the palm of his hand, which was only partially true. Ibrahim Ghamal obeyed him, but Gregory MacPherson had his mind on other things. Now, Greg saw a light at the end of his tunnel. Maybe he would be seeing Lydia soon.

Greg knew what al-Qaeda expected of him. The less he said the better.

In Tehran, Abu Atta saw to the final changes in Ibrahim's/Greg's appearance. He ordered special shoes with lifts that increased his height about two inches. Greg had his hair and beard re-dyed black. Greg was also fitted with brown contact lenses, further disguising the red-headed, blue-eyed American. The diagonal eye to nose scar from his judo-wrestling trial in Kabul, his loss of weight and weathered skin totally changed his appearance. Greg was also issued a professionally made passport as Ibrahim Ghamal.

On the leg from Tehran to Istanbul they both slept. CSA flight # 91 was delayed, so there was enough time to say a prayer in the Blue Mosque and gape at the greatest cupolas on earth: the former Christian church, Saint Sophia, turned into a mosque of Islam.

At the covered bazaar, Abu bought a wristwatch for his *brother* Ibrahim. "You'll need it," he mumbled enigmatically. Then, some new clothes and a second-hand suitcase were purchased.

The next stop was at a Turkish bath, where they rubbed each other's backs and relaxed on the marble floor. Ibrahim left his rags in the bath's garbage and exited the place looking like an elegant young Arab.

Greg was aware that on the way out and back to the airport, they used the cargo terminal, where Abu Atta had lots of friends. No one asked for passports there.

The night flight to Prague had a short stop-over at Budapest. In Prague, their passports were checked carefully, and questions asked. The visa's page was stamped, *For the city of Prague, only!* The *brother's* booked a room in hotel Astorya near Prashna Vrana[1]. Abu Atta slipped two crisp ten-dollar bills into Ibrahim's pocket.

"Buy yourself some lunch," he said curtly. "I have business to attend to."

This time, Ibrahim followed him. He considered himself a good sleuth. It didn't take him long to discover that he wasn't the only one on Atta's tail.

---

1   Prague's Gate, historic monument.

Abu passed by the clock-tower, famous for its figurines, then he crossed the plaza and sat at a table in an open-air cafeteria. Soon a Middle Eastern *businessman* joined him. They shook hands and had coffee and cognac while chatting in a friendly fashion. Ibrahim became aware that someone from a second floor window was taking a number of snapshots of the two men at the table. He walked quickly back to the hotel. It wasn't in his interest to be found out by Czech intelligence.

Was it possible for the Czechs to identify Gregory MacPherson under his darkened beard and moustache? Not likely. He now no longer fitted the description of the Greg MacPherson they would be looking for. After all the dramatic changes to his appearance, even someone who knew him well would not have recognized him.

Then? The "Government of One," Greg MacPherson, had decided—The "Army of One" had to be reactivated! The only question was when and where.

Abu Atta came back late, but he was not alone. He had generously tipped the receptionist and smuggled a couple of classy prostitutes and two bottles of French champagne into their hotel room. Greg hadn't seen anything like it since Beirut. Lydia was a world away. It was a blasphemy even thinking of her. His sex-starved body accepted with gratitude any piece of female flesh, especially a perfumed, good looking European woman. It turned into an orgy. Abu proclaimed it a nice *soiree aux quatre*. He was very proud of his smattering of French.

At four-thirty they left the prostitutes and took a taxicab to catch an early flight to Montreal. Abu Atta didn't die in Prague. His unexpected generosity had bought him more than a nice foursome's night. It also meant that the "army of one" hadn't killed him in Prague as Greg had planned to do. The prostitutes distracted him and later he would be glad, because it could have forfeited his meeting with Lydia.

Ten

The man that arrived with Abu Atta in Montreal wasn't the same Gregory MacPherson who had left Canada a few years ago. Nevertheless, everything that Greg had stashed away hit him like a direct blow to the midriff. He closed his eyes and a flock of memories whirled over him. The humiliations in the *sports club*, the cruel punches to his crotch that he wasn't permitted to return, the subhuman treatment he received from the mobsters. Maybe Abu Atta wasn't altogether off target. That "civilization" was rotten!

Greg's life had been an endless chain of cruelty and rejections. Even his medal he had won as a Marine was nothing but a mockery, an award for killing young men that had done nothing to Gregory MacPherson. And Oklahoma! Those people had nothing to do with him and nothing to do with Waco, Texas.

Perhaps his revenge for things he thought done to him were aimed in the wrong direction. If he had been pushed into it by the very people now craving his punishment—the

U.S. government, wouldn't it seem logical that Gregory MacPherson should be helping Abu Atta. An eye for an eye, a tooth for a tooth!

In the taxicab Abu took his hand. "Are you OK, Ibrahim?" He only partially guessed his thoughts.

Greg opened his eyes, mind boiling with bitterness and unanswered doubts. "I'm fine, *brother*." He forced up a tortuous smile, "Better than ever!"

They rented rooms in a small *auberge* on Munro Street. While signing in, even a perfunctory look at the page informed Greg of the abundance of Arab names. Abu Atta sent him up to their rooms with their bags, while he stayed and met a couple of men that had been waiting for him.

It was a nice day in late summer, though the room's window offered no other view but the gray backs of other buildings. Greg started to pick up the telephone receiver, then changed his mind. He went down and exchanged a Prague ten-dollar bill for Canadian money including coins he would need. He went outside to look for a public phone at least a block away from the hotel. He found one in a department store, and with shaky hands, dialed Lydia's number in Hamilton. On the second ring her father answered.

"I'm sorry to bother you, sir," Greg said calmly as he could, " may I talk to Lydia?"

"She has gone back to college, but I can give you her campus telephone number, if you don't have it." Ian had no notion of the caller's identity and didn't bother to ask.

"I don't have my phonebook with me, sir." Greg was the very personification of politeness. "I'd be much obliged if you gave it to me."

"No problem, but I'm late for work. I'll make it snappy."

"I have pencil and paper, sir." Lydia's father dictated the area code and the number, and Greg repeated it. "Sorry for the inconvenience. Good day, sir."

He couldn't believe his luck, it was a Montreal number. He dialed immediately. She might be in the dorm. Again, he was in luck. Lydia answered.

"It's me, Lydia," he said in his thick, coarse voice.

She recognized him instantly. "Greg, where are you?"

"On Munro and Shanteclair. May I come and see you?"

Lydia was obviously shaken. She thought she had successfully put all this behind her. After his long-distance phone call, she was able to put her emotions to rest. She rationalized that if Greg was able to place a call from Asia, he must be with friends and have access to money. It was then, her father and the doctor saw her improved enough to go back to school, then college. Now, his voice brought back a flood of emotions. For a moment it felt like her madness was taking her over. She finally answered, "I'll see you in half an hour in the bar at the corner of Lafayette and Cronstadt. Do you know it?"

"I'll be there. See you." He hung up and pressed his forehead to the wall, his heart thumping heavily. "So be it," he whispered.

Greg took no transportation. He ran. He ignored oncoming traffic and other pedestrians, and bumped into people here and there. Twice he was almost run over by cars. His emotions ran amok. Was he really in love with Lydia or just imagining he was? Since his emotional upheaval at the Pakistan border, his transcontinental telephone call, the agony and disorientation he had suffered, he had felt both dejected and indifferent. But, one thing was for sure: now he was obsessed with the idea of being in love with Lydia.

Near the cross-streets of Lafayette and Cronstadt, he almost walked away, then he gathered his nerves and strode into the bar.

Lydia was sipping coffee at a small table toward the back, though not the Lydia he had met in Hamilton. The teenage girl had grown to a magnificent young woman of unrivaled beauty. She didn't recognize him under his masterful disguise, but the way he looked around gave him away. She waved him over to her table a bit hesitantly. Greg approached like a sleepwalker, then stopped at the back of the other chair without tearing his eyes from the fantastic vision before him.

"I didn't know…" he started to say, *that you had grown so much*. That would've been stupid. "…if you would really want to see me," he finished clumsily.

Lydia managed a tiny, meaningless smile. "I didn't know, either, but I'm here. Sit down. It is you, isn't it, Greg?" He mechanically sat still staring at her.

The barman came. Lydia took the initiative, "Two dry martinis, unless…" she looked at Greg, he nodded. "That will be all," she said.

The man moved on to other customers. Lydia transferred her dark blue eyes to the busy traffic, then back at the stranger across the table.

"To say you changed a lot," she said abstractly, "would be an understatement. What happened to you, world traveler?"

Greg had forgotten his line, his mouth felt dry. He felt the absurdity of this meeting. It served no purpose. There were chasms of obstacles, chunks of masonry and bloody pieces of human flesh between the two of them. Under the circumstances, to say, *I love you, Lydia,* would've been grotesque and monstrously unbefitting, but these were the only words he wanted to say. He made an attempt to take control of himself.

"This dark moustache and the beard do change my appearance, but I can't stand them. I wonder how you recognized me. I've lost so much weight. You look so lovely." Greg felt sick with the futility of what he blurted out. It hung between them like a wet rag at the end of a broomstick.

Then Lydia stunned both of them. "Five years, Greg—for five years I had thought, struggled to obliterate my thoughts of you." She swallowed hard, "I tried to reason with myself, but it didn't work. The inexplicable feeling remained. Something about your inter-planetary dream and your eternal solitude. Perhaps it was something I read between the lines of your one and only letter to me, Greg. Somehow, I knew how much you needed to be loved, and I really believe there is a kinder, indefinable part of you that I'd be capable of loving." Tears rolled down her face unchecked, "I know all about you and that horrible deed of yours, which is impossible to exonerate or explain, though I cannot tear myself away from you."

She reached across and placed her hand over Greg's. He felt her lovely, kind vibes, powerfully spreading through his soul and body. He seized her delicate fingers. "I'm damned, Lydia," he said gulping down his own tears, "but, if you could truly love me, your love can give me a saving grace. An idea has been floating around my mind for awhile, but it's disconnected and formless. Now, I know what it is precisely. I can do it, Lydia, then you can love me forever, calling me Greg MacPherson. God blesses you, I can do it. I swear in His Name, I can do it. **I can do it!**"

For the first time in his young life, he felt, almost physically, the immediate presence of God. The third person at the table.

In the meantime, Agent Cliff desperately tried to check Lydia's movements, but his Canadian friend didn't return his messages. The big-wigs over him seemed strangely detached.

Over the next few days, Greg and Lydia became reconnected. Fortunately, the days were sunny and the nights balmy, and they were left alone. The Arabs in the hotel were busy planning their entry into the U.S. They were to enter one-by-one at different checkpoints, then join existing cells. Unfortunately, Greg was so busy with the seed of love that had burrowed into him and was growing like a snowball rolling down a mountainside, that he was completely unaware of their plans. His masterful disguise as Ibrahim Ghamal—another Arab among many others—kept him from being rediscovered as Greg MacPherson by the authorities.

Abdoulah Atta took special care that his American *brother* went undetected.

Ibrahim was never invited to the secretive meetings, so he had plenty of time to spend with Lydia. Abu ordered his people to keep an eye on him. The reports were about a girlfriend. Then, of course, Abu remembered Lydia and the long-ago phone call from that remote country. He took his sleuths off the case. Was he pushing his luck? Could Lydia be connected to Greg MacPherson AKA Ibrahim Ghamal?

Abu invited the ex-Marine and Lydia to have dinner with him. He not only wanted to check Lydia out, but also wanted to know about the training of foreign students in American private schools. Greg knew nothing, but Lydia seemed better informed, probably through her father's underground connections. Abu probed further. He asked if Ibrahim had learned how to fly a plane while in the Marines. Greg explained that he had been taught how to operate as second pilot, and that he was aware that a few of his ex-colleagues had become civil aviation instructors, and also that one of them had started a flying school down in Florida. Abu expressed interest in meeting him if he was still there. His dream from childhood was to learn how to fly a plane. This was his explanation to Greg and Lydia, though it sounded hollow and unconvincing.

With Lydia's gentle prodding, Greg had become more able to ponder things and think for himself. He had always been suspicious of Abu's motives. He also was concerned in an abstract way about what would happen to him after the Arab group entered the U.S. It wouldn't be like Abu to leave himself in any way vulnerable. Canada had plenty of flying schools for small aircrafts, but Abu was interested in commercial flying in the U.S. He wondered why that would be. Why was he planning on going to the U.S.? Especially with someone fatally compromised in his country, like Gregory MacPherson. Suddenly, Greg thought Lydia could be in jeopardy as well. Now that was a different matter. It shook him to the core.

What exactly were Abu's expectations of the ex-marine? Of what use was he to al-Qaeda anymore? That was something to think about. Greg thought to himself that he would have to do some research on other possibilities. He tried to imagine a large plan that would cause terrible damage to his fellow countrymen. Not only was Abu keeping things from him, but he was well guarded as well. Two of his men slept in his room and guarded him wherever he went. At this point, Greg flipped back to a state of indecision.

It was a serious mess, and Greg wasn't quiet sure what to do. He wasn't concerned only about himself, but for *him and Lydia together*. He needed to find out exactly what Abu and the Arabs were planning. After the questions that had been asked by Abu, he suspected it was something to do with learning to fly commercial planes. He would have to keep his eyes and ears open but he felt out of focus and lost. Could he trust Lydia? He knew nearly nothing personal about her life.

Gregory MacPherson was released from the Marines on suspicion of *erratic schizophrenia,* but this was kept confidential. The Marine psychiatrists didn't want to admit they had missed this prognosis from the beginning.

An epidemic of unattended cases of erratic schizophrenia had been spreading over the Middle East throughout centuries. It has always been murderous. To those people, religion wasn't a deterrent, just a catalyst. In present times, this syndrome had degenerated into a hydra of unchecked hate against Western civilization, with the U.S. as the Great Satan. What scientists did not want to know was that, *de facto,* the Great Satan wasn't spared either.

Greg was entering a phase of severe paranoia. Since Abu had suggested that Lydia accompany Greg as he re-entered the U.S., he became even more disturbed. He even became downright suspicious of Lydia.

Had Lydia been conscripted into the al-Qaeda organization after the telephone conversation from Afghanistan? Had she been brain-washed? Or perhaps she was operating under direction of an intelligence service such as the CIA.

This last suspicion disturbed Greg more than anything else because it seemed the most logical to him. The more he thought about how easily Lydia and he had slid into a trusting relationship, the more he felt like a pathetic fool. It took someone like himself, hungry for crumbs of love, to be trapped in a voyage of no return. He decided to keep his guard up.

However, the wonderful sex coupled with kind and loving treatment, lowered his guard considerably. The relationship eased his tensions and depressions. He even looked relaxed and happy, though underneath, the pressure constantly mounted, ready for eruption in its own time. In Afghanistan, Greg was closely watched, but in these surroundings, his personal decisions were his only warden and stimulus.

Lydia had an old VW "Bug." They drove it to the hills and the beach, picnicking under the stars, sleeping in a small collapsible tent. Being with a beautiful, *normal* woman was a joy Greg had never before discovered.

Once in awhile, the same suspicions would crop up. Did she really love him? Had she revealed his true motivations? Had she been paid by the Federal Bureau of Investigations or the CIA to bring his defenses down so she could find out what he would do next with his Arab buddies?

In his paranoid state of mind coupled with his voracious need for love, love became a hell as it wiggled its way into his devastated heart. However, sometimes, unexpectedly, even a pretense of love may straighten the knots temporarily.

So, Greg chose to believe that the love between himself and Lydia was merciful, unselfish, generous and unique.

In the last moments of existence, a human might be blessed with a glimpse of eternity, a whole lifetime in a drop of blood. The same could happen in a Great Love. It doesn't matter how long it lasts. It could be a moment, but priceless, absolving, consuming...LOVE ITSELF!

The ecstasy of Love to the death. An instant later it would've been lost, but now he knew what immortal Love was about. It cannot be stolen, sold or exchanged. IT IS FOREVER."

Suddenly, Cliff's Canadian counterpart spoke. A medical practitioner had been arrested for malpractice. Lydia's secret file had been discovered—she was partially insane!

Actually, her physician had written in Latin, *morbidum*—terminal case. Any extreme emotional strain

can preclude most of the global functions in her mind."
Then, as an afterthought he had added, in his hard,
masculine handwriting, the end of an Italian stanza.
"...*comme face al mancar dell' allimento*—can't help the flame
if it's fuel is consumed."

"So," Cliff groaned, "that makes the two of them. God,
help me."

Eleven

Abu Atta was aware of the sudden changes in Ibrahim Ghamal. He saw that his eyes had become cool and calm. Ibrahim was well-focused, and his smile gradually warmed his usually sober face. Yes, *Ibrahim's smile!* Abu didn't remember him smiling at all before.

He took his protégé to lunch in a first-class restaurant. "What's happening, my *brother*?" He asked while lighting their cigarettes, "You look like a million bucks."

Greg's eyes didn't shift as usual, he glanced at the menu with a furtive smile. "I met my great love, Abu."

"That's cool, man," his protector exclaimed. "Lydia is a beauty queen. Even I would've fallen for her, but I'm expendable."

"So am I," Greg declared, inhaling the cigarette smoke avidly. "I'll take the *soufflé* with green onions, cheese and sausage and a glass of Chardonnay."

"Let's make it a bottle," Abu offered generously. "We have a cause to celebrate." He called the waiter, "Two *soufflés de Briton* and a bottle of *Rambouillette* '95."

The waiter bowed lightly and inquired, "Is it a birthday, gentlemen?"

Abu smiled broadly, "It is."

"Then, you get two pieces of chocolate cake on the house." The waiter took his leave.

"Is it your birthday, Abu?" Greg knew he was lying.

"Of course not," the boss laughed buoyantly. "But big things are about to happen. Now we are brothers in the same cause, though things can change at a moment's notice. For now, you are to be my hand-picked companion to your native country. If Lydia can come with us, it would be even better. What do you think?"

"I don't know whether Lydia would want to leave Canada, Abu. I never asked her whether she wanted to or not." He paused, then blurted out, "Is she part of your organization?"

Abu's eyes widened in surprise. "Of course she isn't. Lydia never would have been approached by us. Is that what you have been thinking?"When Greg nodded curtly, Abu said, "Let me tell you a few things about Lydia that you don't seem to know," and he proceeded to inform Greg briefly of Ian's tainted past and Lydia's radical activities.

Greg probably expected it. He didn't manifest any surprise. "Then why do you want her to come with us? Do you want to involve her in your great plan?" Greg asked after a considerable pause.

"Of course not. But since you are in love, you will be happier," Abu suggested.

The waiter served their meals, then poured a bit of the wine in Abu's glass. The young man sniffed at it as if he were a connoisseur.

"*Tres bien, merci,*" he said in passable French, taking a sip, "*oh…ce ça de bon gout,* excellent!"

After filling their glasses the server took his leave with another small bow. The *brothers* touched glasses.

"To the success of our cause," Abu said confidently.

Greg nodded silently and drained his glass. He thought for a moment, then asked, "Am I not to be told what your plans are?"

Abu sipped his wine. He refilled Greg's glass silently, then crushed his cigarette out in the ashtray.

"A *soufflé* should be eaten while hot," he said with a little smile. "Happy Birthday to us!"

The observation deck at the university with the best view over Montreal was empty. They spread a blanket at a grassy spot and stretched out on it.

Lydia, sprawled next to Greg and wove her fingers around his. "Let me come, please. The authorities are more apt to listen to me, besides you wouldn't even be able to talk to them without being captured."

"Who said anything about talking to the authorities, Lydia?" Greg appreciated Lydia's response to his concerns when he told her about Abu's secretive plans. However, he kept to himself the assurance that Lydia would not be able to convince any authority in the U.S. that there was significant cause for an investigation into her concerns. Especially after they checked her background, which they undoubtedly would, and discovered her father had escaped to Canada as a Communist, and that Lydia herself had been involved in campus protests. So far, Abu's information always proved correct. That was the reason why he didn't oppose her coming, and perhaps there was something else unknown to Greg.

He just smiled at Lydia, and then shrugged his shoulders. "I'm not even trusted by the Arabs. But, talking to Abu and keeping my ear to the ground I've surmised a couple of things. Sadam Hussein and his sons might be establishing close business ties with al-Qaeda. Plus when we were in Prague, I saw Abu meet with an Iranian businessman while the local intelligence, who were following him, took quite a few snapshots of the two.

"The meaning of all this is, if I'm not presumptuous," Greg went on to explain, "that something on a global basis is about to come down."

Lydia came up to her elbows, staring curiously at the *Arabian face* next to her. She never thought of Greg as particularly perceptive, but perhaps she had under-estimated him. "Like what? You may not want to answer my question, but I am not anyone's informer...unless I change my mind, and that won't be done without your consent."

"I don't know how to answer your question yet, Lydia," Greg murmured, closing his eyes against the blazing sun. "I'm not the mastermind behind this affair. Atta isn't, either. I thought of killing him in Prague, but it suddenly struck me that it meant nothing. There is a Big Boss conducting his own sinister puppet theater, not a bit like yours. The blockbuster is that the U.S. and Canada have just a fraction of an idea what could be coming, and judging by the TV commentators, it would seem that the new president in the White House is stubbornly ignoring any intelligence."

Lydia crumbled onto the blanket. "My God! If you're right…! If only we knew for sure what is happening…"

Gregory MacPherson felt extremely vulnerable. He openly confessed his misgivings to Lydia, "I am in a dangerous position, Lydia. I, frankly, don't know why I'm with Abu, why he really brought me to this point or what my position is in his intermittently scheming mind."

Lydia nodded, "To tell you the truth, I've wondered about that, too."

He gathered her gently in his arms, "I wouldn't be entrusted with any details, you know. I'm going to have to ingratiate myself further with Abu—do you understand? I think he is somehow addicted to me. Also, you must know that my life, moral and physical, must be forfeited to do what I must do," he whispered.

"Why?"

"Because, I will not be pardoned for what I've done."

Lydia held him close and promised, "I'll be there for you, Greg. We will see this through together."

"You can't understand, Lydia. What I know are only ill-fitting odds and ends of something monstrous." He went on explaining, "What if the Arabs discover I am a traitor to their cause? They might keep you as a hostage against me."

"You do whatever you have to do in total disregard of *my* life," Lydia said firmly. "Even if my head is cut off. Don't do anything half-way, darling. You've convinced me that we must stop them and…"

"Wait a minute, Lydia," Greg cut in. "I want you with me but not part of whatever I have to do."

Even though she had her doubts about Greg's stability, she wanted to encourage him. It was the only way she could help him succeed. Plus, she wanted to reinforce his subconscious hope that this was a way to redeem his terrible deed.

"Let's live in the now, Greg," Lydia insisted. "I'll stand by you to the last."

Lydia's words inspired him. "I swear to God and you, Lydia, I'll do my best to the very end," he asserted without any pathos. "I have just one condition. Don't look at my death if you happen to be around. Please, remember me, as I am now—loving you with all my heart and soul."

Unexpectedly, Ian was fired. The office stated flatly that he was drinking on the job. He had always done it, so why now? He wouldn't be able to pay Lydia's tuition. Now he had to depend on the answer from the U.S.—a scholarship at Boston's university.

How much did the Americans know about his past and present?

Twelve

Upon arriving in Florida with Abu, life in their small cell became hectic.

Lydia, under Greg's guidance, found the flying school and charmed ex-captain O'Malley, one of the two founders of "Fly to Freedom!" He was given the impression that she was the candidate and processed her application immediately. Then, Lydia feigned being called back to Canada, *a death in the family*. She didn't ask for her advance payment to be returned, instead she asked O'Malley to allow "a friend" of hers to take the lessons instead. It was Abu Atta. His desire was to learn how to fly large, cargo planes. He finished paying the whole tuition in cash to seal the deal.

Captain O'Malley e-mailed his partner, who was looking for a money loan in New York: *Saved by the bell, come back—O' Malley.*

He rehired one of the instructors that he previously had to lay off. Their new client was an Arabian on a student visa, filling his summer vacation with action and fun. He spent money like crazy on night spots and prostitutes. Otherwise, he was intelligent and polite and learned quickly. He was sponsored by a good Saudi family in Tampa. It crossed O'Malley's mind to run some background checks through the Pentagon, but those clearances took a hell of a long time. He'd receive them after the client was gone. Besides, the Saudis were trusted allies, especially after Operation Desert Storm. Plus, most important to O'Malley, the Fly for Freedom needed the money.

He was so grateful to Lydia, that he offered a free flying course to her Arab boyfriend. Ibrahim Ghamal accepted it with certain reservations. O'Malley had no idea who Ghamal was. This was reassuring to Abu and Lydia.

Lydia's father, Ian Grey, was of Scottish extraction. In his student years, he became involved in a communist cell that was infiltrated. He had to flee on very short notice with what, literally, he had on his back. On his way to Australia, he got stuck in Canada with no money. Ian was a good, self-taught mechanic. That saved his ass. Otherwise, he kept his university background buried. However, his communist ideology followed him. He was anchored in Hamilton, where he resided, and was made into a sleeping mole.

Ian went to a university campus, one of the communists' cleverly covered-up meeting places, and there he met Lydia's mother. Her name was Clotilda and she was ten years his senior, maybe more, but an established scientist and regular professor of astrophysical engineering. They became further acquainted when he made some repairs in her apartment and left a lasting impression. Ian was handsome and physically fit. Clotilda found him a steady job as a mechanic on the campus. It wasn't long before Ian Grey moved in with her. In the course of a month, they were married. Meanwhile, Lydia was already in progress.

Clotilda had had two failed marriages, but this one held. She corresponded with her other children, but not with the ex-husbands. Ian couldn't care less. He was so cocksure in his performance that possible rivals didn't worry him a bit. He wasn't exactly in love with Tilde, but had a healthy respect for her.

Perhaps that kept their marriage solid. Ian now moved in higher social circles. He had short-lived liaisons with some pretty students, though generally he was loyal and appreciative of his wife.

Gradually, his attachment to Tilde grew into full dependency. She was capable of smoothing any messy situation he was caught in, so Ian felt obliged to her. He thought that was as good as love.

Tilde was constantly preoccupied with her classes and scientific research, so Ian found a nanny to feed Lydia. The rest he did himself. Tilde got pregnant again, however, she miscarried at seven months. The fetus was a boy. The doctor put his foot down—no more babies. Tilde was overage and another pregnancy could be fatal.

In his lighthearted way, Ian brushed it off easily. "Too bad."

Subsequently, in her troubled conscience, for as long as she lived, which wasn't very long, Tilde had dreams of her unborn boy growing to be a man.

Lydia was 10 when her mother passed away. Ian took it very hard. He had lost the pillar of his life and turned to excessive drinking. Inebriated, he would tell Lydia the story of her unborn brother and the dreams of her mom. Lydia was a lonely child. She kept on imagining her brother as her constant playmate. To her, her brother was as real as life itself. Her father doted on her, but Lydia didn't confide in him. She never told anyone about her "ghostly companion."

Then, one rainy morning, the doorbell rang. There stood the brother she had pictured in her imagination. She had only a vague idea that her dad was connected to a radical, underground escape route, and that the young man that stood in her doorway was a fugitive from justice. She fell in love with this image of her brother. Gradually, this obsession grew bigger than life, then became her only reality.

As time went on, Ian became more dependant on his daughter, and when she moved to Montreal to attend college, he turned into the shadow of the man he used to be, leaning entirely on his old friend alcohol for solace, support and energy. It gave him nothing but despair.

In the fall, as Lydia's relationship with Greg was in full swing, Ian received the approval of Lydia's scholarship to a U.S. university. That was a great relief to him. He didn't have a steady income. He called her dorm in Montreal. Her roommate said she was out on field trip. As there was a deadline for a response to the letter, he insisted that Lydia return the call as soon as she came back.

When there was no response, Ian called Lydia's counselor. He was informed there was no field trip! As much as Ian hated to do it, he turned to his underground connections. They told him they would check it out. Four hours later they called back. It was an operator he knew by name—a man called Dante.

"I don't know if you wanna hear this, Ian."

Ian's heart sank to the pit of his stomach, "Shoot."

"Lydia is keeping company with two up-to-no-good Arabs somewhere in Florida."

"What do you mean by no good," Ian whispered.

"As possible terrorists, they are being trailed by the FBI and the CIA. We can't help you."

Ian recovered his voice. "Help me personally then, Dante, please. You have a daughter…"

"I can't, Ian, as much as I wish to…" now it was Dante's turn to whisper, "No one in his right mind would fool around with terrorists or get mixed up with the FBI or CIA. No way."

Ian was crestfallen. "What can I do? She's my only child."

"Well, I can't help you any further, I don't even know where in Florida your daughter is. That's it."

Ian slammed the phone into its cradle. He'd have to have a stiff drink to figure out what to do next. Damn, Lydia, what had she become involved with?

Lydia and Greg were followed.

It wasn't clear who was doing it, though it was a fact. Today, while Abu was currently busy learning to fly, Lydia and Greg lay on the warm white sand in their swimsuits, gazing at the surf. It was the only place they felt it was safe to talk.

"Do you think Abu Atta's intention is to hijack an American airliner?"

Greg shook his head. "That's a possibility, but he wouldn't have to necessarily learn how to fly one—they'd just force the pilot at gun point. Abu is too smart for that. I just know that whatever is being planned, it certainly involves learning to operate American planes."

"You told me Abu wants to become a martyr. That is what frightens me. Plus, another thing. You said you thought a few of his other Arab friends wanted to learn to fly commercial planes as well. Is that something you can probe Abu about?" asked Lydia.

Greg first looked at her in a disoriented, confused way, then stared at the angry surf as if the answer was written in the waves. "I only know bits and pieces, Lydia, and I've told you this. I read between the lines when Abu vaguely talks about his plans to me. Well, I will try to find out more." the frustrated young man continued, "but who wants to know?" His voice was unusually harsh and raspy.

Lydia pulled back from Greg, talking to him in a no-nonsense tone, "You once said to me, in order to stop a plan from taking place, you must remove the snake's head. But this can't be done until almost *zero* hour, otherwise the snake could be replaced." When Greg avoided her eyes, she grabbed his chin and moved his head to face her. "You said the head is supposed to start the action, otherwise the rest won't know what to do."

Looking at Greg, Lydia wondered if he even remembered he had said that. It seemed as though only part of him was there. His mind under stress had been fading. His need for narcotics quadrupled.

In total frustration, Lydia slapped his face, saying, "What's the matter? Are you listening to me?"

Suddenly, Greg grabbed her hand, his eyes sparkling angrily. He twisted Lydia's wrist painfully. "Don't ever treat me like that again! I'm not a child," he hissed venomously. "First, I've got to talk to Abu…"

It was then that Lydia spotted the man who had his eyes on them. He was partially covered by the trunk of a palm tree. "Quit whispering like an idiot," Lydia screamed, feigning great anger, but she was actually scared. "No one is listening. We are all alone by the Atlantic!"

Greg followed her eyes, jumped to his feet, running toward the overfed, *beach-boy*-type agent who had a powerful listening and recording device that amplified whispering, even from some distance away.

"Get out of here—leave us alone!" Greg shouted angrily. He may have been a little smaller in stature, but he was ready and able to take the guy on.

"No way," the intruder smiled brazenly. "This is a public beach, not an Arab's property."

"Listen, you shit, I'll make you swallow your listening device, and your pearly whites along with it!" Greg roared.

The muscleman's sultry smile spread across his face, "Try it, you little Arab bum." His presence at the scene had probably saved Lydia's life. She was fully aware of it.

Greg drop-kicked him to the sand, then sat on his chest earnestly trying to push the device down his throat. "Swallow it, you bastard. Swallow it now, scumbag!" he ordered mercilessly, forgetting to fake an Arab accent.

Lydia tried to stop him but she was too late. The guy's teeth were gone, his mouth a well of blood. She thought to herself that his medical bills were covered by the FBI.

Lydia pulled Greg back in the direction of their towels. Greg cast the agent's bloody listening device far into in the ocean, then sat down next to her, trying to catch his breath.

"I want to marry you, Lydia," he murmured in rhythm with the surf, "if you'll take me. It's a bad deal; you deserve something better than a jackass like me."

"Who will you be?" Lydia asked, deeply perturbed, her wrist still hurting. "The young man from planet Vegha 77 or Greg?" Now that the first rosy blinders were peeling away, she dreaded the thought of marrying him, but her love-fear for him was overpowering. Besides, Lydia knew his paranoia could ruin everything if he doubted her feelings toward him for a moment.

Greg smiled broadly, "Both."

Lydia smiled lovingly at him, but actually, she was filled with nausea as she pretended to tease him, saying, "I don't want to be accused of bigamy. Name just one…"

"It's your call," Greg mumbled, taking her in his mighty hug. He had forgotten his deadly anger. "Why are you so good to me? Were you always saving homeless dogs and cats?"

"Not a single one. I just lost my mind over two men at one time."

Greg bristled, "Who's the other one? Abu?"

"Good heaven's no! " she laughed again. "Anyone but Abu. It happens to be only you and your parallel self from Vegha."

Great relief brightened Greg's face and made him appear handsome with great sex appeal. "I'll smother him if he keeps on butting in. What do you like about the guy on Vegha?"

"His honesty coupled with loyalty," asserted Lydia. "He is always generous and kind."

"He's crazy, Lydia."

Grimacing from the pain in her injured wrist, Lydia put her hand over his lips and said, "No, darling. You are the crazy one, but I love you all the same. After all, I'm crazy, too, you know."

Greg bit her fingers lightly, "So, I am the lucky guy! Did someone hurt you, darling?"

"You…," she giggled, "stole my heart, you thief." Lydia decided this was the time to open up about what she had suspected and recently had confirmed. It would dispel any doubts Greg had about her feelings for him. "And you're the father of my child."

It worked! Greg was dumbstruck with the news. "Is the baby boy the reason behind your decision to marry me?"

"*She* certainly is."

"How do you know it isn't a him?"

"The doctor says so."

Greg shook with anticipation, perspiring profusely. "You've already gone to see a doctor?"

"Of course. I have to protect myself and the precious being growing inside me."

Greg felt dizzy with joy, but asked for more. "When did you go to a doctor?"

"Yesterday. They did an ultrasound and they gave me her picture."

Greg roared like lion, his mind reeling, "How old is she?"

Lydia caressed his bushy dark beard. "Old enough to be yours. I'm not a scarlet woman, you should know that by now. You are my handsome Arab. Your disguise is perfect, but now I'm sure we are being followed round the clock."

Greg had a sheepish expression painted on his face. "Do you think I've been recognized?" Lydia nodded her head.

"How do you know?" Greg asked with his brows furrowed with a worried expression.

"I think the answer is because of your Arab disguise. Many middle easterners have recently entered the U.S., and I'm sure the Secret Service has been put on alert."

Greg was still unable to grasp the situation. "And you still want to marry me?"

"More than ever," she told him as she also wondered if she had another choice. Now she was frightened of him, though, surprisingly, her fatal attraction toward Greg was growing at an alarming rate.

It took him no more than a minute to come to terms with her answer. "Let's go back to our room, my dearest Lydia. I'll carry you in my arms."

Lydia's laughter rang in the air, "Why? I'm a faster runner than you. I'll beat you to the motel. Wanna bet?" But her heart was choked by a faceless, sinister premonition. *What's next?*

Thirteen

gent Cliff finished swimming his laps, dressed by his locker and walked energetically to his office. However, even after a long swim his bad mood persisted. This morning his altercation with Lora had almost provoked their breaking point.

"Don't tell me," she said with mockery in her voice, "that you're the only one that can settle the case of those Arabs in Florida. Everyone seems to be getting paranoid about terrorism."

"I wish that was true," stated Cliff taking his coffee cup to the kitchen.

Lora followed him, starting to rinse off the breakfast dishes. Cliff took a cigarette out and she looked at him disapprovingly. "Not again."

Cliff threw the cigarette in the trash container and after a short hesitation, the whole package. "One of those guys may be Gregory MacPherson," he went on to inform Lora.

"How do you know?"

"I don't know. It's just a hunch."

His wife shook her head. "You haven't talked to your daughter yet. Her teachers asked me if I'm separated."

"Pardon me, but I don't believe that, Lora."

"What's the difference?" she mumbled evenly while turning the dish washer on.

"What's the difference of what?" Cliff was losing his patience.

"If I am married or divorced," Lora finished. "You're always absent. It may be because the weather here is turning bad, and Florida is warm and cozy year round."

"Don't forget the hurricanes, Lora."

Lora stopped shortly before leaving the kitchen and retorted sarcastically, "Oh, come on, Cliff, of course not, I've seen them on television."

Greg and Lydia were married in a quiet civil ceremony in Las Vegas where it was least likely to attract attention. Lydia became one very disturbed Mrs. Ibrahim Ghamal. She was shaken to the core by the incongruity of this marriage. She just took more Xanax. As a wedding present, Abu Atta paid Lydia's entire credit card bill and gave them fifty thousand dollars in cash.

Was it truly a gift or hush-money for rendered services? Lydia accepted it and opened an account at Chase Manhattan under the name of Lydia Ghamal—they had both agreed to that. It could be her protection in the future.

While the newlyweds were honeymooning in Orlando, Florida, Abu finished his flying courses, then joined them at the Disney extravaganza, a celebration of life at it's best in a make-believe way, a dream world built to whisk one away from reality. It didn't matter if it was the only time or the last time. In the grand scheme of things, life could be just a dream, and the awakening is the only moment of truth.

Abu Atta was spending money like there was no tomorrow—because there was no tomorrow. All three of them were drunk with the pleasure of life and drugs as if they were creatures from another planet who had suddenly discovered Earth.

Lydia worried about her prescription medication running out because she was unable to renew it in the U.S. without giving herself away. She didn't want to ask Abu for the drug either. That would be just one more hold he would have over her.

She tried to read Abu's mind. Did Abu Atta believe that Allah would grant him a palace with a thousand maidens? Not quite. As a sophisticated man of the world, he knew that martyrdom doesn't pay. However, his suppressed, barbaric mind wanted its own freedom, to destroy the civilization unattainable for his disadvantaged race, to humiliate and shatter to smithereens the secure, comfortable life of western people—the nonbelievers.

Otherwise, for his brothers and sisters, tomorrow was as bleak and joyless as any other day. The barbarian age shall return to earth, then everyone will stand on equal terms facing Allah and his prophet.

Though, before that time, Abu Atta wanted to savor anything the *perverse* western culture had created, losing himself in sexual orgies, drugs and amusements, until he stripped away all vestiges of civility, down to the perennial beast he was, turning his back on his own principles and religious convictions.

There had never been a tomorrow that he had looked forward to, and now his tomorrows were dwindling down to zero.

Agent Cliff openly shadowed Lydia almost around the clock. She was the weakest link and he expected to break her.

In the meantime, Lydia's father was freaking out. After he hung up from Dante, his underground contact, Ian never felt so hopeless and lost. His beloved daughter had taken off without informing him. *It just wasn't like her.* She knew how much he needed her love. In fear and frustration, he took to the bottle. Hours later he awoke from his drunken stupor to a voice telling him to look for Lydia. He didn't know where.

Ian rushed drunkenly from room to room, ending at the broom closet. She wasn't in there. In a blind rage he destroyed every bit of her puppetry. Then suddenly, it came back to him. His underground connection had told him she was in Florida!

Ian took the first available flight to Miami, imagining all kinds of horrors happening to his beloved daughter. The Canadian whiskey in his flask went down well with the black coffee served on board, meals he turned down. He had no idea where in Florida she could be.

At Miami International, it really hit him. Where was he to go now? He tried Dante's number again. No answer. Dante had prattled on the phone with Ian and, obviously, it wasn't appreciated by the bosses who had recorded their conversation. Ian tried numerous times to reach him but, no dice.

Ian started looking for Arabs. He found not a single one. He consumed the last drops of his second flask and there was no more. He had to visit the airport bar. The ambience was semi-dark, with discrete lights and soft music. He grabbed an empty stool and leaned on the bar, eyeing the few customers. Abdoulah Atta had been just about to board his flight after seeing one of his cell mates off to another destination with some last minute objectives, when he decided to have a quick drink. He took a seat at the bar, just as Ian was eyeing the customers. Ian spotted him. Damn, there's an Arab! Young—somewhere in his twenties—sharp features, thin lips, the athletic type. Without a second thought, Ian moved next to him.

"Do you mind?" His tongue had become fat and unwieldy with liquor. "I hate to drink alone."

Abu Atta looked him over. A spare, well-trimmed individual in his late forties or early fifties. There was no doubt that he had had one too many. "What's up, pops?

What do you want from me?" the young man snapped, far from friendly.

Ian was taken aback a little bit. He had addressed a total stranger, but in drinking holes that was considered acceptable. However, he was too drunk to worry about manners and politeness.

"Maybe you can help me. My only daughter eloped with an Arab. They were accompanied by an Arab friend," he stuttered. "I wonder if you know them."

Surprisingly, the stranger smiled, not friendly, but with a degree of indifference.

"Allah is great! I certainly do know them."

Ian spilled his drink and searched for his glasses. He put them on and looked at the Arab up close. "You wouldn't kid me, would you?" he whined pathetically. "It's a matter of life and death!"

"To you?" Abu laughed. "I'll take you to your daughter."

Tears spilled from Ian's bloodshot eyes. "Will ya?"

"Honest to Allah, I will. Do you have baggage?"

"No, I don't…not even a toothbrush. God blesses ya, you're saving the life of a father."

"Don't mention it," Abu mused. "Now you have a son and also a granddaughter in the making. I'll drink to that." He finished his drink in one gulp.

"I do, do I? How's Lydia?" Ian was shocked.

"Lydia is thriving. Let's go. The flight is boarding, and we have to buy you a ticket. I'll treat." Abu walked out briskly, and Ian had to work to keep up with him, "Thank you, sir. I can't believe my luck! And a baby on the way! Am I dreaming? It can't be my Lydia."

Abdoulah Atta didn't bother to answer him. There were enough empty seats that they could sit together, and he guided the drunken man to one next to the window.

"Where are we going?" Ian asked anxiously.

"Do you want another drink?" Abu asked, ignoring Ian's question.

"No…I better not." Ian admitted, "I'm getting sleepy. I just want to see my Lydia again."

Fourteen

Greg and Lydia felt they were being watched all the time.

Who was doing it was hard to define—the terrorists? Government agencies? Maybe both?

About midday towards the end of the week, Lydia was alone and desperate, unable to concentrate on shopping. She decided to take a big chance and approached one of those men she knew was following them. He was in the parking lot of the shopping center. The man was clean cut, smartly dressed and sitting behind the wheel of a standard model Ford with the windows open. He wasn't exactly handsome, but seemed intelligent and alert, just entering middle age. Lydia made sure they were not being watched.

"Show me your badge, please," she said without preamble. The agent accommodated her. "Where can we talk, Mr. Cliff?" she asked after checking his credentials.

"Go back to your car and unhook the hood," the agent offered efficiently.

Within a short time, he joined her and opened the hood pretending he was looking at the engine. Lydia leaned in with him, "Something terrible and super big is about to take place, Mr. Cliff," she murmured in his ear. "Something of unforeseen proportions.

"I am now married to Ibrahim Ghamal and he is trying to integrate himself into the confidence of the other Arabs. We only know they are planning something terrible and that planes are involved." She glanced over her shoulder and saw nothing alarming.

"Any proof?"

"No proof. But we know it's al-Qaeda. It is well-planned and meticulously hidden. There are cells spread throughout the U.S." Lydia moved to the other side of the car. It gave her a better line of vision.

The man moved after her. "Though I'm relatively high on the totem pole, no one would believe me without facts, ma'am."

"I can present some vague leads, but I'm afraid no facts." Lydia's nerves were on edge, her hands trembled and perspiration bathed her face. The day was unusually hot and muggy, even for Florida. She wiped her face and went on bravely. "Just don't try to stop my husband and I will try to get more information to you."

"Why? Why are you doing this? To throw suspicions from yourselves?"

"No, by no means," she tried to explain. "My husband hates al-Qaeda—for humiliations they inflicted upon him. To him, it's a personal vendetta. He is a deeply disturbed human being, Mr. Cliff."

"Why do you say that?"

Lydia was struggling for words. "I'm talking about a split personality," she sighed. "But please, just keep an eye on us, not arrests as yet."

The agent peered into her troubled eyes. "I cannot promise anything, Mrs. Ghamal. We have been wary of the sudden influx of middle eastern gentlemen entering the U.S. That is why we are following all of you. Now, what you are telling me is very serious."

"Please," begged Lydia, "let me keep you informed so that you can step in at the right time. You have nothing on Abu Atta. He has no criminal record in this country. His entry was legal under his real name." Lydia was desperate, "Don't come too close to us, either or the others will grow suspicious."

The agent banged the hood of the car shut. "Alright, I'll see what I can do. No promises, but call me if anything moves." He gave her his cell phone number.

Cliff went back to his car deeply concerned. His instinct told him Mrs. Ghamal wasn't lying, but then how much of the truth did she really know? The Canadian trace on her had been confirmed. Her father had a deeply tainted past. She could be perceived as a double agent. Cliff's shirt was glued to his back, over-saturated with perspiration. Rivulets streamed in his eyes. His brain felt like mush. Two *urgent* messages flashed from his dashboard unit. One from home, another from a local police agency. He had asked to be alerted about any unusual local crimes.

In spite of the heat, Greg, clad in his swimming briefs, methodically did his strenuous daily workout on a little grassy spot next to the motel. Dripping with sweat, he ran lightly to the car, opening the door for Lydia. Eating well, being in love and getting plenty of sleep had done wonders for him. With his short military haircut and his beard shaved off, he looked boyishly handsome and athletic—the classic "boy-next-door." He took her in his sweaty embrace and kissed her hungrily.

"I still can't believe I have a wife of my own," Greg laughed happily. "I must be dreaming. Pinch me!"

Lydia thought briskly, *Is it possible that Greg is capable of erasing from his mind the pending doom, living only in the NOW? Is it due to his psychotic state or was he simply born that way?*

She snuggled close to him, taking in his male aroma. She tried to imagine that this strong protective body of love could disappear instantly, nowhere to be found. *Forget about saving people and their self-made hell*, she thought feverishly. *I want him alive!*

"Let's runaway, Greg," she pleaded with him desperately.

"Run…where?" Greg asked holding her chin up, looking intently into her deep blue eyes.

"Anyplace!" She insisted foolishly.

"Anyplace? There is no such place, Lydia, and you know it." He said it without the tiniest presence of bitterness. "If I have a choice, I don't wanna die in any other fucking place but home. All other countries just stink, I've been there. Here one can drink and eat decently…work…find himself a girl to love…have children. Of course I forfeited that part, but that was my own fault—nobody else's. This country has nothing to do with it, nor anyone else to blame. I damned myself and that's that! Case open and closed."

Lydia was stunned. *Is it remotely possible that Greg's mind is functioning?* She locked the car, pondering his words. Actually, that was the longest speech she had ever heard from him.

"I've been wondering, Greg," she began to voice some of her doubts, "why does Abu Atta trust you, of all people, with his life?"

Greg had a ready answer, "Because, he is positive I will never report him to the police or the government of any country on the globe. I couldn't without exposing myself. He fights his holy war, I fight mine. We will fight each other to the death, but not in the open. It will be our private war."

Lydia felt like screaming, but she tried to calmly reason with Greg. "Wait a minute, Greg. You know his intentions are against this country, and all you want is a barehanded, private war? You don't make any sense. Do you need him for something more than his money we are living on?"

Greg seemed suddenly distant, "Listen, Lydia, as much as I love you, there are some things I am unwilling to explain even to myself."

Lydia felt sticky and smelling of perspiration. All she craved was a cold shower.

She walked to their room, followed by Greg, then stopped at the door and abruptly turned on him. "Really? Is it possible that Abu is in love with you?"

Greg's face expressed almost infantile wonder. "In love with me? You must be joking!"

"No, I'm not, Greg, it does happen. Especially between *brothers*. You are now of the Islamic faith, aren't you or…haven't you thought about that, either? You may be surprised, but I have some thoughts, too. I thought you would pass through hell to prevent Abu's murderous plotting. I was willing to share with you the humiliation of being a slave to this infernal monster." Then she lost control. "Now you are telling me there are things you don't want me to know? If that is the case, I've fallen in love with the wrong man. I think you need Abu for another reason as well. For now, I don't want you to cross over the threshold of this room. We cannot talk inside anyway, you know we're bugged."

Lydia stopped her barrage of angry words to take a breath, then she realized how utterly defeated her husband was. He looked like a dog beaten nearly to death by his master with not the slightest idea why.

"Don't shut me out, Lydia, please, " he pleaded pitifully. "Just tell me what you want, and I'll do it."

Lydia was distressed by the discovery that she still loved this infantile man that she called "husband." He certainly was more a brainless child than a male in his prime and glory. The realization that she had married him in the name of Love, "till death do us part," and was having his baby, made her knees seem to melt out from under her. She had to sit down by the door. Greg knelt next to her.

"I have tried to be honest with you all along, Lydia," he moaned.

She looked at him with pity, suddenly facing the truth, "You've missed your fix, haven't you?"

"In this country, the damn stuff isn't always readily available." He had tears in his eyes.

"Good God, on top of everything else, I'm sharing my life with an out-of-control junkie," she muttered as if to herself. "Go and do your push ups and cartwheels until your 'savior' returns."

"Don't hate me, Lydia, I love you," Greg pleaded.

She picked herself up from the cement with a deep sigh and walked into their room, closing and then locking the door in Greg's face. With trembling fingers she found the pill box in her purse and gulped her last two Xanax tablets without water. "From one junkie to another," she murmured to herself.

The buzzing in Greg's head had started again. He was unable to think on any level. He had just lost the best thing that had ever happened in his damned life, and was utterly unable to fathom how it all deteriorated so suddenly. He renewed his stretching exercises just to keep busy.

Abu Atta drove into the motel parking lot shortly after eight p.m. Greg joined him on the way to his room. "What am I supposed to do for Allah's sake, Abu? Lydia has locked me out. She won't even talk to me."

They walked to Atta's room. Abu closed the door firmly. "You are in bad mental shape, *brother*," he hissed, pushing a lion's dose of hash into his trembling hand. "Take this, then we'll talk."

Greg devoured the narcotic and threw himself on Atta's bed in near agony. He was torn by horrendous spasms, the room spinning madly. He felt he was on Vegha 77, the protective bubble badly punctured, the air rushing out with incredible speed. Was it time to go to the edge and jump into the void?

Gradually a steely calm spread over his body and mind. Abu had taken a shower but hadn't rubbed himself dry. He approached Greg's bed naked and staring at the beautiful body stretched out before him. With a lizard's smile, he straddled the spread-eagle man and grabbed his hands.

"You are pinned, Ibrahim," he laughed lustfully. "Weak as a kitten. You won't even simulate a token of resistance, though actually you won this round. I can't part with your body." The man released his hands, lit a cigarette and blew the smoke in Greg's face. "You look much better without your disguise. A beard doesn't look right on you." He took another deep pull of nicotine. "I cannot function normally without your physical presence. Arabs only pretend discipline. And at its core, discipline means to us fear and fanaticism. Against all the rules of iron discipline bestowed on us by Osama, I'm taking you to New York. I must examine the fucking towers firsthand."

"It's OK with me," Greg muttered. "But I won't go anywhere without my wife."

Abu shrugged his shoulders, "Let her come with us."

"But I told you, she wants to leave me, Abu!" Greg exploded.

Abu was infuriated, "Triple cursed, fucking bitch!!" He got out of the bed, pulled on a bathrobe, then adjusted his bulky erection. Lydia was closing the door, suitcase in her hand. Atta pushed her brutally back into the room.

"Nobody walks out on me and lives!" He shouted, face distorted with rage.

Sensing mortal danger, Lydia paled. "If it's the wedding ring…"

"Keep the damn ring!" He was nearly hysterical, but kept his voice down, "Your place is next to your husband, or I'll cut your head off. That's Islamic law. I paid you a lot of money and now you're trying to sneak out right from under my nose? Death to you!"

Lydia had never faced such horror as she read her death sentence in Abu's reptilian eyes. The young woman dropped onto the bed, horrified.

"We are leaving tonight for New York," the demonic man hissed again. "That means you, your pitiful husband and I are leaving in one hour. You will come with me now to my room. Greg is there. Keep your suitcase."

She followed him, shaking like a leaf.

Lydia looked around desperately for an escape route as they walked to Abu's room, but he had a tight hold on her arm. When they entered, she couldn't even look at Greg. She walked directly into the bathroom and locked the door. It was hot in the confines of the small bath and the light was dim. She pulled open the shower curtain thinking a shower might help her think. A naked male body hung from the shower head. *It was her father!* The vision dissipated in front of her eyes. She couldn't even scream as she fell to the floor. The cool tile finally revived her. To her chagrin, after that vision, even the company of Greg and Abu was more appealing than staying in the abominable bathroom. She had sold herself to Satan.

Cliff had called home, returning the urgent message. His daughter was critically ill. He would have to get there as soon as possible, but first, he called his contact at the police station. There always was a chance for a lead. What he heard perked up his instincts, and he decided to check it out, hoping the local police wouldn't think he was interfering.

After introducing himself, the officer in charge was cooperative with Cliff.

"Let me read the police report to you, Mr. Cliff. 'A nude male body washed up on the beach, not in his prime but well preserved, obviously hasn't been long in the water, and he is not a local. Marks of strangulation on his throat, no rigor mortis yet. No other marks on the body except for an indentation, possibly from a wedding ring, on the third finger of his left hand. The indentation indicates that it had been worn for a long time. No trace of a struggle. The man was drunk, probably unconscious. Murder is the educated guess. Death occurred about two hours ago. Dead before being thrown in the water.' "

Cliff pondered the information and almost asked if there was any identification before remembering the body was nude. Then he asked to be informed if they came up with anything that could identify the victim. He asked, "Could I see the boddy, officer?"

The officer called the coroner and Cliff drove over to see the remains. He was stunned. Ian Grey had been under surveillance because of his communist connections. His face was on file and now his body was on a slab in the morgue.

There had to be a connection to the Arabs and what was going to happen—it could be a lead to what Lydia had told him. He called the police and suggested strongly that they arrest the Arabs staying at the Boca Vista Beach Motel.

"On what charges?"

"False identity! Anything! Call my cell phone or Headquarters. I'll be quite a distance away, headed back to D.C. on a private emergency."

He drove like a madman to the airport and caught a flight to Dulles airport.

A few hours later, Cliff stood by the phone in his Washington D.C. home. It was eleven-thirty p.m. and his little girl, Glenna, had pneumonia—temperature 106. The doctor was expected any minute now. He hadn't heard anything from the police in Orlando.

He checked on his daughter. His wife was firmly posted by Glenna's bedside. Cliff decided to make a quick call to the Boca Vista Beach Motel himself—perhaps he could even reach Lydia. The police could wait. He dialed the number on his cell phone. A woman's voice answered.

He identified himself and asked if there had been any police action.

"Yes, Mr. Cliff. The police are here now. Want to talk to them?"

"No, ma'am. Just answer me…are the Ghamals still there?"

"No sir. Mr. and Mrs. Ghamal along with the other Arab in room 40A left for the airport a couple of hours ago."

Cliff let his breath out in frustration. Lydia had cheated him. He pocketed the phone and ran to the computer. The last flight out of Boca-Raton was to New York, Kennedy airport!

The next flight to New York from Dulles was in thirty minutes. The doorbell rang. He opened the door to let the doctor in. At least knowing his daughter would be taken care of permitted him to concentrate solely on the case. He left "the father" in his house—"the agent" was the only one needed on the job.

Cliff ran, grabbing a jacket on the way out. He jumped into the family car and sped off to the airport thinking there could be many, many lives at stake. In flight, he alerted the CIA of what might be happening. They said they would check the airport and try to put a tail on the trio.

Fifteen

On the red-eye flight to Kennedy International, Greg and Abu seemed normal, or what normalcy meant to them. Lydia was seated between the two men, far from calm. She was wide wake and still shaking. She was ill prepared for the onslaught of new developments. There was no way to get in touch with Cliff or any other operator for that matter. The plane phone was out of the question. She was afraid of even suggesting a visit to the restroom. Her nervous system was thoroughly shaken, especially after the vision of her father. What was the meaning of it? Of course, she had progressively abandoned him—knowingly so. His dependence on her after her mother's death was total, in stark disregard of her privacy. A man of his age should be capable of taking care of himself. Lydia had lied to Greg. She hadn't mustered the courage to inform Ian of her marriage. Suddenly she felt awful about it. Why was she so complacent until this specific moment?

She felt something horrendous was about to happen. She glanced stealthily at her two companions—Greg, her husband whom she bitterly realized was the biggest mistake of her convoluted life, and the fully evil presence of Abu Atta.

Her husband was manageable, and his *brother* icily polite. Neither of them talked to each other, so she didn't know if the "big bang" was now, tomorrow or in the course of the next few days. She desperately tried to come up with some feasible possibility. Was Greg going to act against Abu Atta upon arrival, later or never?

The lights were dimmed and most passengers were asleep, the rest yawning with relaxation. There were quite a number of suspicious faces. Three were of Arabic extraction, one was praying. If Lydia screamed to attract attention she would only be asking for more trouble, maybe even hurry the looming disaster.

Then again, it might not be tonight.

Greg placed his hand over hers, "I love you, Lydia." He whispered and she felt the return of her desire. He was in full possession of his faculties—instincts under control. She took a deep breath, fighting to restore her equilibrium. With a sudden surge of confidence, she nestled her head into Greg's chest. "I love you, too, darling, I don't know what came over me."

Abu Atta smiled almost humanely. "You know, Lydia," he said softly, "I'm not quite the religious fanatic you think me to be. Deep inside myself I firmly believe that the souls of the dead don't go to hell or paradise. From here they are transferred to an enormous junkyard planet where Allah bestows life to the soon-to-be newborn. There, He picks parts from the discarded souls. That way nothing is lost. In the process of creating a brand new being, the old is reborn. However, the new and the old never coexist peacefully. We inherit the sins of many past generations, in the hope that we can do better. More often than not, this intent remains only wishful thinking. No one gets a mansion and a thousand beautiful maidens. Torn by inner strife, we squander everything, though Allah will never be bankrupt. He is the Horn of Plenty."

Lydia tried to unbend a little. *Whatever happens, it won't be tonight*, she thought to herself. "Could we change seats so that I can be on the aisle?" she politely asked Atta.

"Why not?"

They shifted seats.

"Thanks, Abu."

One of Abu's cell phones rang. He answered it speaking colloquial Arabic. He made it short, then pocketed the phone. Greg threw a sharp glance at him. "What corpse?" he asked in English.

Abu laughed dryly, "A friend lost his old cat. It has been found."

Greg knotted his eyebrows, "Really?"

"Would I lie to you over such trivia?"

They exchanged murderous glances.

Greg hissed, "You are a compulsive liar, Abu."

"Does that make me more of a murderer, brother?" Atta hissed back.

The two savages were ready to jump at each other's throat. Lydia was alarmed. She knew they could be arrested and that would prove nothing as far as the impending threat was concerned. At this point, police detention would be ruinous to Abu's plans, so he would appreciate her intervention.

She straightened up. "Please, Abu, leave the boyish stuff aside! You guys better behave yourselves and not attract attention." Then she asked to be excused to go to the restroom.

The reaction of the two protagonists was surprising. Greg tried to hold her back, but Abu pushed him aside. "My bodyguards don't trust you, let me take care of it."

He led Lydia down the aisle. "Soon I'll split that thick head of your husband. You deserve someone better," he whispered in her ear.

Lydia chose to play this game to the hilt. "But you love each other, Abu."

"That's true," Atta laughed. "Though love has little to do with our paranormal hate for each other. The next time around, I'll get rid of my guards, I give you my word of honor. Me and him—one on one." He pressed her slightly against the restroom door, "Will you be mine?"

Lydia thought hastily, batting her eyes, she murmured in a surprisingly amorous voice, "Yes, if you shake off your guards. They make me awfully nervous."

Her dad was right, she was a born actress.

At the airport, Abu Atta made good on his word. He sent his three bodyguards on a fool's errand.

From Kennedy Airport, he, Lydia and Greg caught a taxicab and asked to be taken directly to the World Trade Center complex. The driver pulled away from the curb, shrugging his shoulders and saying, "Who do you expect to find in the Towers at this time of night? Ghosts or terrorists?" he asked with a silly grin. "Why don't I drive you to a nice hotel," the cabby offered this with a hacking cough. "Do you mind if I light a cigarette?"

Abu agreed and treated everyone to his cigarette holder. Lydia, of course, refused. Abu used the car's lighter. "You are right, we'll call you back later." Atta was familiar with taxi drivers' habits. "Stop at that Starbuck's. I'll buy coffee for every one and make a couple of phone calls."

"What for?" The man would lose other fares. "Use my phone. We can survive without coffee, can't we?"

"Thanks, but no thanks." Abu laughed like a hyena, "Do as I say and you'll be tipped generously."

The cabby shrugged his shoulders again as he pulled up in front of Starbucks. "It's on your bill. I was just trying to help, but I'll do as you wish."

"Good thinking, maestro," Abu quipped. "I'll be back in a jiffy."

Abu ordered regular coffee with cream and got busy on the public phone instead of his cell. His call was answered immediately.

"Good morning, cousin. I'm sorry to bother you so early. The dummy that I am, I lost my keys." He listened shortly, "In a black pouch, the alarm included...you keep the code in the restroom as usual...I know. Give me the number of your credit card...Great, I love you, brother."

He dialed another number. "Are your power doors activated? You changed the linen, great...aha...same as usual, thanks, a million."

Abu took the cardboard coffee tray to the car, served the cups and disposed of the tray. He then said to Greg, "Good, old uncle Hassim. He sends you his love and many blessings."

The cabby sipped on his coffee mumbling, "What's this? I like it black…Say, boss, your folks are coming to the Big Apple in droves. Is it a holy week or something?

"It's a hospitality week, brother," Abu answered politely in the New York lingo. "Would you slow down a bit? We try to stay away from cops."

The cab driver nodded, slowing for a minute or so. "I know what you mean, brother." He winked conspiratorially. "Check me out, I'm clean, but if you brought some 'candy' I'll buy, cash only." The brakes screeched, tires hissed, the cabby hollered through the open window. "Fuck you, son-of-bitch…go back to California!" It was a near collision.

Abu wrote a number on the back of a phony business card—*Harroun Al Rashid & Sons—Haberdashery*—and handed it to the obnoxious hack. "Call this number and say, *I like them hot and steamy.*"

The driver beamed, sticking the card in the band of his uniform cap. "I will. I thank you!" He didn't overcharge them but took the tip.

"Do you want me to wait, boss?"

"No. Just drop us off at the back of Tower Two and be blessed with a million."

The middle-aged cabby displayed all his gold caps. "I'd sooner drop dead, than harm you. Here's my card, if you need privacy. Break a leg, folks."

The underground parking door, under Tower Two North was left ajar as Abu had been told it would be.

It was too early for the towers to be opened, but Abu Atta had a key to one of the private elevators that went from the parking garage to the top of Tower Two. Lydia was locked in a private waiting room on the twentieth floor, while the two men traveled to the top. Abu knew the combinations to open all of the doors. At the top of the tall building, the doors slid open noiselessly, no alarm systems activated.

The helicopter pad looked eerie wrapped in the foggy embrace of early morning clouds.

Knowing the two Arabs and Lydia were now in New York, Cliff had no doubt something was up. However, the FBI and CIA refused to cooperate on such nebulous proof. Cliff heard from the men posted at the airport that the cab was driving the suspects to the World Trade Center. Reporting of this provoked only a feeble reaction from his CIA boss. Two young men and a girl heading to the Towers could just be going into work early. What's the danger?

"We don't know if they are armed or unarmed," Cliff shouted. "But, I swear to God, that *girl* is the woman who contacted me. She is Mrs. Ibrahim Ghamal, and we have been watching Abu Atta. Lydia Ghamal is a Canadian, and she promised to call me if something was on the move, but she didn't. I'm thinking she could be in trouble as well."

"Cool it, Cliff!" ordered the suave voice, but some interest was clearly detectable. "Why would Atta be acting alone? Wouldn't he mobilize his network?"

"How can you be sure he didn't, sir?"

"Since you alerted us, we were able to tap in on his cell phone. He hasn't made any calls. Not yet."

Cliff's voice was getting rocky with despair. "Half an our ago, a cabbie mentioned something about droves of Arabs arriving in New York. I don't know what this Abu Atta is cooking up, but it must be the World Trade Center again," Cliff croaked as he wiped perspiration off his forehead.

The CIA big shot remained adamant. "Listen, Cliff, we are simply going to wait and see what happens—what they are up to. Terrorists won't hit an empty house." Cliff leaned on the wall, silent, eyes closed, heart thumping in his mouth, "Hey, Cliff, are you there?"

Cliff answered dejectedly after a pause. "Yes, I am, but I don't know why."

"Drop it, Cliff. You are doing a great job. Just keep it up. I'll give you the chief's number. Wake him up, then if nothing happens, guess who'll be held responsible...me! You'll take a leave of absence. As usual, don't write this number down, memorize it!"

Cliff dialed the number given him. The man answered at the fifth ring not quite lucid. "What the hell...five in the morning! Who is this?"

Cliff told him. The chief was dripping vinegar, groggy. "So, the World Trade Center has *reportedly* been penetrated, and I don't know about it? Is that so?"

"It looks like that, sir."

"Alright, alright. I'll be there by eight."

"Chief, I need to be there now, and I need some backup."

"What the hell are you talking about?"

"Will you authorize me to call them, sir."

"Do you know how serious this is, Agent Cliff, whoever you are?" The man was blowing his nose.

Cliff paused, then said, "Of course, I do."

There was silence on the line, then the chief's voice came out grudgingly, but loud and clear. "Go to the World

Trade Center's night-shift officer. Show your credentials, I'll call ahead for you."

The fabulous view from the heliport of tower number two was invisible. No matter how much the two young men strained their eyes, everything was concealed by thick, gray clouds. Away, farther north, the lights and the outlines of the top of the Empire State Building were barely discernible. Even the breathing of the great city was congested by the fog. A light, chilly breeze visited from the ocean. The gloomy, mournful fog horns of maneuvering ships provided the only background sound. The tops of the twin towers, with their long array of signal lights hung over nothingness, blinking like space station terminals lost in bleak infinity—like Vegha 77—at least Greg thought so.

Abu Atta's face wore a strange, cadaver-like grin, which made him look like an ancient, theatrical mask.

"Your blast at the provincial city hall, Greg MacPherson," he announced in a derogatory way, "will look pitiful compared to what will happen here. These monstrous symbols of power and money, made of plate-glass and steel will disintegrate to smithereens, collapsing down to their very foundations. The whole economic structure of the invincible American oligarchy will follow suit—the *greatest nation* on earth, on its knees, begging for pity. No one has succeeded in this, but I will!" His upper lip trembled with triumphant pride, "Allah has hand-picked me for this immortal glory!"

Greg laughed scornfully. "You have in mind Osama Bin Laden, my *brother* Abu. What are you but one of Osama's slaves, a tiny junior lieutenant. I was the only mastermind of my crime and my abettors were nothing. They were just a mention. My deal was mine only, though now I wish I had never done it. If you brought me here just to brag about what will happen, forget it. I'm ashamed of what I've done. It was a total attack on my ego, fed by a vanity not unlike your *glorious* palaver. God never inspires the miserable raging of egomaniacs. In this deed of yours you'll be all alone and invisible. Allah won't even use you for spare parts."

Abu Atta hissed with venom, "When I give the signal with this cell phone—my men will start the process. They will take over a designated plane at Logan Airport. Then, you, Lydia and I will die together as they aim the plane into this tower. That will be my entrance to glory and you will be with me to witness it."

Greg laughed hoarsely. "You are lying, Abu. It won't be tonight."

Many floors down, Lydia was agonizing. Now, she realized why Abu Atta wanted Greg alone on the roof. He had to brag about his project to someone to get an immediate reaction to enlarge his already berserk ego. Obviously, Abu was going to die in the process as a *martyr*, but a martyr that had seen his sainthood. He had to impress someone important (to him), but disposable, because all witnesses should be killed. That included her, as well. Abu's intelligence was sharp but shallow. To him people were inferior garbage. Persons of his kind could be efficient only in the hands of the Bin Ladens of this world.

However, Abu Atta's vanity required tokens of admiration, even if only for scant moments. He saw no risk in it; or was it that the risk made it sweeter to him?

All lines of communication had been cut, the waiting room she was in was locked electronically. Abu had taken her cell phone. She felt totally helpless. There must be some way to help and stop whatever was about to happen. But how? Feverishly, she tried to find the alarm system, but saw nothing like that in the room. She was so frantic that she was paralyzed. She sat on a chair, not one muscle budging, her voice mute, her brain blocked. She tried to force herself out of this almost comatose state.

If only she had been able to contact Agent Cliff. Lydia had kept alert to get the word out, but there had been no opportunity to even try and reach Cliff or any other help.

In trying to think things through, Lydia suddenly thought of her mother. She had missed every opportunity to become really close to her. Well, not totally. Through her, she felt she had met her unborn brother, and Greg had seemed to be in his very image. She had been drawn into a vortex of something enormous and unpredictable. She hadn't hesitated to love Gregory MacPherson because of that.

Hell, no-o-ooo! But it is never too late. She remembered the brave fight her mother put up with cancer up to the very last moment. Her agony was awesome, the pains excruciating. Lydia thought of disconnecting the life support. Her mom was aware of it. She found the strength even to smile. "Don't do it, dearest. I still may have a fighting chance, please, don't destroy your personal karma for my sake…" she murmured.

"I can't take it, mom!" Lydia sobbed. " Your pain can't be alleviated."

Nevertheless, her mother's last words were, "*My brave little soldier, I wish I could see you as a grown young woman. Your dad needs you, but don't lean upon him. Your father is helpless—find your own strength.*"

Was Lydia capable of helping anyone?

The world might be in need of her, and this tiny girl growing in her womb needed her, too. She would be their spacebridge to a new life.

Involuntarily, her eyes fell upon a large mirror. In it, she saw two dear images—*her mother and father in a solid embrace.*

Suddenly she broke free of her impasse. "God, give me strength!" She cried out.

Lydia was strong and athletic. With uncommon force, she grabbed pieces of furniture and threw them at the reinforced glass of the partition…again and again!

The alarm went on, high pitched, like a desperate scream for help!

Sixteen

The guard's quarters in the World Trade Center was ablaze with pulsating red lights. Cliff held up his credentials as he glanced at the monitors. "Twentieth floor, Tower Two!" he cried out.

The officer double-checked, "I have a patrol on the fifteenth floor. I'll send them up!"

Agent Cliff suddenly shouted, "Forget *Morgan Stanley* on the twentieth! It's not a burglary, the attack might be coming from the air. Send them straight up to the heliport on Tower Two instead! And call for air reinforcement!"

The man looked at him dumbfounded but turned to raise the alarm.

Someone had disabled all the elevators. Cliff ran up the steps with a number of security officers right behind him. It seemed an endless, hopeless run against time.

TIME! How much time did they have?

Every step was like a day in Cliff's life that flashed before his mind's eye. He prayed that his daughter would survive his inconsistency as a model father. He was never of any help to his family anyway, except monetarily, probably because he wasn't made that way. He was just a robotic agent and nothing else.

What had happened to Lydia? Was she still alive? She was last seen at Kennedy Airport with a double escort, Atta and a strangely subdued Ibrahim Ghamal.

Cliff had read the report on Lydia sent from Canada. She had lost her mother to cancer and she might be part of the leftist underground like her father who had a proven radical record. Was it possible that she had become a traitor? All leads pointed in that direction. Lydia's eyes were honest, but perhaps she was a good actress.

Cliff's heart seemed near the bursting point. He was losing momentum. The younger men bypassed him. He wasn't young by any standards, though still in pretty good shape. Farther, faster…up and up… He prayed they would be on time, but for what!? And for whom!? He prayed for this and that, but was someone listening to his chaotic prayers? Was he a human being?

Police cars raced wildly toward the Twin Towers—lights flashing, tires screeching—traffic swinging left and right. Finally, the big shots caught on. Calls went out everywhere, the White House, the Pentagon, the FBI.

Suddenly, the night was filled with signals. Signals from the good guys—signals from the bad guys—and prayers, prayers, prayers—prayers from everywhere.

In the foggy morning, two military helicopters scrambled toward the WTC-2, and due to poor visibility, almost collided. Then, a signal light flashed out a coded order, *Do not land on Tower Two!*

"Why not?" asked one of the pilots over the radio.

"People on top."

"So what?"

"They're fighting," was the short and cryptic answer.

The captain turned toward his second in command. "What do you make of this?"

The lieutenant shrugged his shoulders. "Some nuts have lost their marbles."

The younger man sounded sure of himself. "It can't be an attack of any kind. Terrorists' tactics are different."

"Who knows what the terrorists' tactics are?" the captain mused.

The lieutenant was confused. "Maybe…we shouldn't land. It could be mayhem. Damn fog!"

"Lieutenant, turn on your night-vision goggles."

It was hard to out-shout the noise of the engine. "I can see without goggles, Captain. Two men are rolling around on the tarmac, dangerously close to the rim…."

The Captain tried the night vision. "It looks like a street fight. Why on the top of the WTC-2 of all places?"

"Who knows?" the lieutenant shouted back, veering over the platform. "We don't have to risk our necks just to break up a single fight."

The other helicopter called for orders and was told, " Let's just hang here and see what happens."

He tried the Security Office in the building. The commander wasn't available. His secretary had no explanation why the two men were fighting each other. She saw on the monitor that there was someone in the *Morgan Stanley* suite breaking stuff. It could be an unrelated incident.

The captain waved his large hand, repeating his previous order to the pilots, "Hover over. Stand by…this could be a false alarm…"

"Wait a minute, Captain!" His co-pilot cut in, "Check out the radar!"

The captain peered at the screen, "Looks like two small aircraft—civil aviation planes or maybe choppers. They appear to be flying up the coast, following the shoreline. God Almighty! There is no radio contact, and they're both only two miles away and seem to be approaching Manhattan. Let's verify the situation, Lieutenant." Then he ordered the other helicopter to keep the watch.

Headquarters called. "Unidentified small planes—could be some crop dusters reported stolen. They are approximately two miles southward from you. They have not contacted for permission to be in that air space. Flight originated probably south along the Atlantic coast. We have reason to believe they intend to drop poison canisters—possibly over Manhattan. Stop them over open water." The captain repeated the order to his gunners.

Greg and Atta abruptly stopped their fighting when Atta's cell phone pierced the air. In their well-trained military minds, it acted like a referee's whistle. "I told them not to call me here, unless my private line has been broken into." He was hesitant.

Greg hoped it would prove to be an *act of God*, a way to stop Abu from carrying out his perfidious plan. "It could be an emergency...an extreme emergency," he suggested, struggling to restore his breathing to normal.

The Arab nodded and put the cell phone to his ear. "*El Harroun Haberdashery* here."

The voice was somewhat familiar. "Are you with father?"

"As usual," Abu confirmed.

"We are two drivers short."

Abu listened tensely then abruptly asked, "Where?"

"In Mecca."

"What happened?"

"Short."

"Stand by. I'll be there as soon as possible." He pushed the phone in his pocket. Abu's sharp mind made instantaneous decisions. "Damn!" He turned to Greg. "You are more than a brother to me, Greg. Forget my bragging, forget our fight. Will you come with me?"

Now—Greg knew—it was an act of God. Abu looked at him as he had back in the past. "Where?"

"Wherever we must be."

"Where?"

"Boston."

"What about Lydia?" Greg asked tentatively.

"She should be fine here. She just doesn't know enough. I have rented a small plane to be available in New Jersey for emergencies like this."

Greg laughed derisively. "Like all the big shots of this world, you thought you could get away, didn't you?"

"I did," Abu mumbled. "There was a slight possibility. Not now. Will you come?"

Greg looked sharply into Abu's dark eyes. "Do you trust me, Abu?'

"We could die fighting each other or fighting for the same cause. Lydia doesn't love you. No one could love jerks like us. But, we can die together. I don't mind living with you on Vegha 77." Then he added, "You cannot have a new start, Greg."

His former *brother* shook his head in a way that could have been read as *yes* and *no*. "But I can have a new end, *brother* Abu. Think about that. Let's get out of here before the building codes are restored."

Finally, the guards reached the heliport doors. They tried feverishly to unlock the heavy metal doors. Combinations had been changed and there were no locks to shoot open.

The voice of the commanding officer yelled over the walkie-talkie, "Take them alive!"

The patrol commander pointed his middle finger at his walkie-talkie in total frustration, "What? We can't even get through the doors, you idiot." He spoke *sotto voce* to his companions.

At the twentieth floor, the patrol guards had problems with the door code to the *Morgan Stanley* offices. By now, the control panel had told them that one lone woman was raising the havoc. It was unlikely that she had a bomb, but still it was possible that she could activate explosives by cell phone. However, why would she create the havoc in the first place, if not to attract attention? Maybe she was trying to draw their attention away from the heliport. The moment they managed to open the door, Lydia flew out in stocking feet, hair flying in disarray, shouting hysterically, "Get up to the heliport—Now!"

Because police cars from all precincts coming from different directions to surround Tower Two, early morning workers gathered to see what was happening!

The cops tried to hold them at bay, because there was no telling what harm could befall the bystanders. But the crowd kept on growing. Is it another bomb? Where is it? The cops didn't know any more then they did.

Speculation became wild. It was a giant oil tanker. A dozen witnesses swore to God they saw it with their own eyes. No-o-o, it was three yellow cabs breaking through the barrier. Someone else offered that he had seen five black balloons coming from the ocean, hiding in the fog. They could be filled with poisonous gas. Still, the curious people gorged on panic and bloody scenes. More humans had died of curiosity than any other lethal disease.

The towers were invisible, veiled in the shrouds of the thick fog. The ever tempting anticipation of *what's gonna happen* was palpable in the air.

Then, the sounds resembling an in-air gun battle came to their ears. They heard dull explosions preceded by blue lightning in a southward direction from the towers and out from shore.

Finally, the crowd was seized with panic by the sounds, though no one was moving away. They had no clue that they had just been saved from breathing poison from the air. They still waited to see what would happen next. But the *next* in this case was the *great unknown*.

Agent Cliff watched the guards attaching a small detonator to the plastic explosives that had been placed at strategic points over the heavy, lined steel door. The security screens hadn't been focused on the fight, but Cliff thought it was deadly. The security men didn't seem in a hurry to finish the work; it had to be precise.

One elevator car arrived, disgorging a special-forces unit charging ahead with heavy machine guns and a horror-stricken Lydia who refused to be held back. She was incoherent.

She grabbed Cliff's lapels with the force of total desperation, "I couldn't get to you—you've got to stop them!"

Detective Cliff shouted to the men ready to burst through the door, "Don't shoot! Hear me? Do not shoot!"

The sounds of an intensive gun battle in the air made everyone apprehensive. The explosions shook them, but that had come from a distance.

The explosives on the door were now almost ready to be detonated.

When the door to the platform finally exploded open, they burst through, shouting, "*Freeze*!!!" The heliport was empty!

Lydia was sitting across from Agent Cliff in a cubicle of a room not unlike a prison cell, with a dazed look on her face. She left the empty paper coffee cup by her chair.

She was totally exhausted. She just wanted to lie down and close her eyes—have everything just go away. "That's all I know, Agent Cliff," she said in a whisper. "My brain feels like mush."

Cliff finished his coffee, squashed the paper cup and threw it into the trash basket. "But you still love Gregory MacPherson." He fought the desire to light a cigarette, dog-tired himself. "Why?"

Lydia tried desperately to concentrate. "I wish I knew…I'm his wife, bearing his child, am I not supposed to stand by him?"

"You set off the alarm by throwing heavy pieces of furniture at the glass partition," Cliff stated for tenth time.

"So I did," Lydia nodded slowly. "I'm getting fuzzier and fuzzier because I've run out of my prescription drug."

"I sent for it, but you have to cooperate with me." Cliff wished he could shake his nagging headache.

Lydia buried her face in her shaking hands. "I told you, they're going to hit the towers."

"But they didn't." Cliff grimaced as a sharp pain shot down his neck, then tried to gather himself. "I'm in the doghouse with all my bosses. Rumors of a cover-up have spread over the city. The media's switchboards and computer lines are blazing like mad. People want to know what's happening. Two light planes have been destroyed over the bay. The pilots' bodies have been retrieved but not identified yet. The name of the company that rented those crop dusters is phony, its account, as well."

Lydia mumbled, "That sounds like Abu Atta. Maybe the cab driver will know something."

"The son-of-a-bitch has disappeared, but we'll find him," Cliff assured her. "You still believe the terrorists will hit again?"

Lydia wiped her face with a used, crumpled tissue. "If Greg doesn't stop them."

Cliff was incredulous, "Just by himself?"

"He has always acted as a *one man army*."

At this moment, something clicked in Cliff's mind—he understood MacPherson's mystery. They were soul brothers—the Good and the Evil.

The cabby called by the fugitives kept up a constant stream of chatter. Abu and Greg didn't listen to him. They had enough of their own problems to think about. He gave them a fast ride to the private airport in New Jersey and was paid well for his service. He touched the business card tucked in his cap while smiling broadly. "Mr. Harroun Al Rashid! Good luck!" Actually, he thought they had stolen something from WTC Tower II.

On this side of the bay the fog wasn't as thick and nasty as over Manhattan. The light Cessna aircraft was reserved for Mr. Ibrahim Ghamal. Greg threw a glance at Abu, who shrugged his shoulders. "I hired a couple of other planes in my name." MacPherson knew that was another lie. Abu wasn't short on false IDs.

Greg presented his passport with a grunt. He was well-versed on Atta's tactics. The night employee wasn't very curious. He hardly glanced at the pilot's permit and the number of hours in the air, then wrote down the name of the off-shore insurance company.

A mechanic led them to the light aircraft, checked it out and saw them climb in. "It's foggy," he mumbled, "but it's your business."

The plan took off easily, it was practically new. Atta did everything according to the book but didn't turn on the radio. Greg had the map on his knees. Even with the heater on, he felt icy cold. "Boston is north of here," Greg informed Atta.

"Light a cigarette and calm down, dear *brother*. I'm flying out of the harbor." He pointed toward Manhattan and two small planes over the harbor. "We don't want company, do we?"

As they watched, two military choppers flew alongside the two small planes and after a few minutes they opened fire. Abu decided it was time to become scarce, he opened the throttle for more acceleration. The engine whined but did gain speed.

"Those two little planes, my *brother*, were crop dusters—unloaded," Abu laughed mirthlessly. "They were just drawing attention away from us. And what a joke on them—the military will have some explaining to do to the media."

"What excuse do we have?" Greg asked, closing the map.

"We don't need one before Boston."

Greg lit a cigarette. "You think we're gonna reach Boston in this toy plane?"

"We have plenty of time, *brother*." Atta explained patiently, "Today is only the seventh of September."

"So?" Greg said curiously.

Changing the subject, Abu said, "Don't worry about Lydia, Ibrahim. The investigators have nothing against her, and she will give them confusing information."

"Except for the name Ghamal. You made the rental in my name."

"So?" Abu giggled. "It's a most common Arab name. Besides, as you can see nobody is tailing us."

"We didn't make radio contact," Greg argued.

"Someone did, Mr. Ghamal. It was arranged. Especially after downing our empty crop dusters." Abu boxed his shoulder. "Stop worrying, brother, we're fine and dandy. The media spread the word that you and I are in the United Kingdom, I made sure of that!"

"What about the cab driver?" Greg killed the cigarette in the ashtray.

"What about him?" Abu shrugged. "They need time to find him. Besides the *authorities* will be in hot soup now. False alarm. By the time our taxi driver's body is found, he won't be able to tell any stories."

Same day, leading U.S. newspapers, television stations and the European media exploded:

False Terrorist Alarm in New York.

Two civilian planes downed BY MISTAKE.

Who will be the next CIA victim?

Mad Canadian woman triggers panic in New York City. What's next?

In a rental car, Cliff's cell phone rang incessantly. He wasn't answering. "Where could your husband and Atta be, Lydia? I snatched you from the psychiatric ward because you've got to help me or they'll put me there, too."

Lydia shivered in Cliff's raincoat. "I just pray that Atta hasn't killed Greg."

"He hasn't," Cliff rumbled. "They've been seen together." Offhand, he said, "I wish you could connect with him telepathically…"

"I could try," Lydia said in all seriousness.

"Well, then try, it's a life and death situation."

She closed her eyes and whispered something, then murmured, "A name…the name of a city…"

"What city?" Cliff was losing patience.

"Boston, now I'm sure."

"Then we go there!" He stepped on the pedal.

The day was brilliant, not a shred of a cloud. A number of private vessels were spread close to the shoreline fishing. Greg was hungry. "Are we near Boston?" he asked.

Abu laughed. "We aren't going to land at Logan airport."

Greg looked around. "Where then?"

"Nantucket."

"That's an island."

"I hope so," Abu quipped, "and large enough for an airport. Have you ever been there?"

"Never. Martha's Vineyard is supposed to be a playground to the rich and mighty from this area," Greg reported.

"Bravo!" Abu exclaimed. "There, we'll change 'horses.' This one seems to be almost out of gas."

After a successful landing, Greg watched while Abu hot-wired a Toyota. Greg felt that in order to thwart Atta's plan, he had to stay in his *brother's* good graces. So, when the car's engine turned over, he said, "Great, man! You are a genius," though he thought, *any jerk could've done that*.

Abu laughed huskily. "I knew you were gonna see it sooner or later. Are you acting?"

"No way," Greg shook his head. The car left the ferry-boat parking lot and entered the freeway. "I was too ignorant to appreciate someone of your magnitude."

Abu glanced at him a little warily. "I wonder if I can really trust you, bastard."

"Try me in the name of Allah."

"How? I need you one way or the other," Abu hissed. "I'm one man short. First, I have to find a public phone."

"There's a sign, *Food and Lodging Next Exit*," Greg announced.

The phone was in the mini-mart of a Shell station. Greg joined Abu with two cups of black coffee. Abu took one of the cups and let him stay while he made contact. "Hello, uncle…I found a new best man for the wedding. We'll find you at the church—same arrangements, same time. Move on."

Cliff had to show his badge to the traffic officer.

"Speeding in an unmarked vehicle won't take you far, sir. You'll be stopped at each zone. Let me drive you."

That sounded reasonable. Lydia and Cliff abandoned the rental and sat in the back of the police cruiser. The officer turned to him. "Where?"

"Logan Airport. As fast as you can. It's a national emergency."

The car blasted off, lights flashing.

Cliff dialed his boss who answered on the first ring. "The President is pretty angry at the Bureau, Cliff. You are to be suspended."

"The false alarm was a decoy, Roger. The real thing starts in Boston. Reinstate me or we're all lost."

"Who told you about Boston?"

"Mrs. Ghamal. She's with me."

The big shot was horrified. "Damn it, Cliff...you kidnapped her!"

"She came of her own volition. No rights violated," Cliff explained.

"Let me talk to her."

Cliff passed the cell to Lydia. "It's a matter of life and death for many, not just my husband's life...what?...my passport number?...I don't have it. Atta has it. I'm in a police car! Here," Lydia said as she handed the phone back to Cliff.

There was a slight pause, then the voice on the cell phone croaked, "Okay, National Emergency F47—I'll get you clearance. We'll set things in motion again! You know I'm putting my own head under the axe. I'll say a prayer. Good luck."

The cruiser zipped ahead.

Abu Atta made a turn into the parking lot of a fancy hotel-restaurant. Neither one of them was dressed and shaved up to code, but the *maitre d'* found them a discrete table away from the other patrons. Atta made up for it by ordering wine and a meal fit for kings.

"You know, Brahim, that this may be our last supper as well," he announced touching Greg's hand lightly. "Let's make it pleasant. Don't eat your heart out about Lydia. She never loved you except as the visible presence of an unborn brother. The rest is camouflage. Women are more pragmatic than us. What they know best is how to make themselves desirable."

The appetizers were served along with the drinks Abu had ordered. For the first time, Greg realized that he would never touch Lydia again. The realization was so painful and shocking that he grimaced.

Atta read him wrong. "Sudden death doesn't hurt, *brother*."

"To me, death is deliverance. Lydia will be much better off without me."

Their cocktail glasses produced soft, tinkling sounds. Abu smiled almost like a human. "So, you accept martyrdom."

"Wholeheartedly. Your cause is my cause," Greg said. He had to be careful, Abu was smarter than him.

The young Arab brought his eyebrows together. "You can be my co-pilot. Will you accept?"

They sipped their drinks in silence, then Greg replied, "If I'm treated fairly."

"You have been treated fairly," Abu objected. "Your response was inadequate."

Greg gulped the rest of his drink and fell on the appetizers, then he looked seriously at Atta. "Allah is my witness, Abu. You've proved wiser than me. I'll take undisputed orders from you."

Atta finished his drink. "Allah be blessed, we are all his children. You have no other choice, *brother*. I bear no grudge against you. You have been befuddled. It's natural under the present circumstances. Lydia tried to swindle you. She is actually employed by the CIA, no doubt about it. I got that information recently but didn't want to hurt your feelings," Abu lied, trying to chain Greg's allegiance to him.

"I have no other loyalties but to our cause and Allah." Greg fell in step. "Lydia is nothing to me."

Abu was sexually aroused, which combined with the alcohol, muddled his sharp mind. "We'll kneel in front of Allah hand in hand."

Normally, Abu was just moderately devoted to his personalized religion. Now, faced by inescapable death he embraced total fanaticism. In Greg, this process was reversed.

Lydia was within him. He felt her presence and talked to her at will, though he had no notion if it was happening for real.

The main course arrived, lamb chops along with sparkling wine.

Gulping his wine, Abu reminded Greg, "We'll drive the car to the shopping center parking lot, Brahim, and call a cab from there."

Greg attacked the lamb chops. If ever he had his last meal to order, this would've been it. With this thought, he acknowledged that this was his last formal meal.

"Do you think we are followed, *brother* Abu?" Greg asked.

"Not if you haven't told Lydia."

"I haven't spoken to her," Greg answered, his mouth filled with the delicious garlic French bread.

Atta pierced him with his reptilian eyes. "I hope you haven't for your own sake."

"My own sake?"

"Your immortality, *brother*."

Immortality on Vegha 77 was nothing but boredom, thought Greg. He said no more.

Cliff and Lydia were in the office with the Chief of Security at Logan International.

"What are you saying?! National emergency?" His eyebrows flew up. "No one has told me anything."

Cliff attempted to be patient and clear. "I'm telling you now. You saw my papers and you can cross check with my superiors. There is no time to waste. We can't wait for the FBI." Cliff pushed his coffee aside. "They never get involved until it's too late…" he bit his lip. That was a fat blunder on his side.

The Chief of Security smiled maliciously. "Better late than blundering on all levels. When do you expect the hijackers to invade us?"

That was downright idiotic, even as a joke, but Cliff had to keep cool. "Probably at any time in the next 48 hours."

The security chief laughed again. "Do you have any idea how many flights land and take off at Logan?"

"It's your job, Chief," Cliff concluded straightening up to his feet, "I can only warn you. It's something of colossal proportions."

A secretary brought a fax. Cliff sat back down as the chief glanced at it. "The White House cannot make up its mind. The President is not in residence."

Cliff looked at him with sarcasm. He rose from the table again, this time motioning to Lydia to do the same. "And they don't know how to find him. Too bad. The President's Air Force One could be an excellent target too."

The man jumped to his feet. "Where are you going?"

Cliff faced him calmly. "To tell you the truth, I'm too tired to think. I need some sleep."

"You and Mrs. Ghamal could share one of our guest rooms."

"We'd need two rooms," Cliff said with a little smile, "we are not married to each other."

The security officer nodded. "I understand, it's an apartment with two bedrooms."

Cliff shrugged his broad shoulders. "Oh…well, we will certainly take you up on it in that case. I hope you realize how serious the situation is. Throw every available man into this operation as soon as possible. Forget about the White House.

The apartment was certainly adequate. It was getting late but the air traffic was still in full swing. In spite of the sound insulation, the vibration and the noise were still quite strongly felt. An airplane meal was served to them—better than nothing.

As they sat down to eat, Cliff probed Lydia for some answers. "You don't have to answer my question, Lydia, but how in the world could you have fallen for a guy like Gregory MacPherson?"

Lydia stopped eating and looked at him seriously. "Don't expect me explain it, Cliff, but I love him. It's love and fear at the same time. What kind of love that is, I have no idea. I haven't experienced any other kind. It may be due to my chronic mental state. Greg is going through his own *crime and punishment*. I still believe in him—he will try to get even with the evil part of himself so his daughter and I can remember the man called Gregory MacPherson with something akin to Love."

"You are going through with having this child?"

"Yes, if the fetus survives my physical and emotional condition."

Cliff reached out and touched her hand, "If it means anything to you, I actually do understand, at least partially."

"How am I supposed to help, Cliff?" Lydia responded.

"With all due respect to your personal feelings," he tried to concentrate, "you're the only one that can pinpoint Abu Atta and Greg in disguise. The pictures on their documents are misleading."

Lydia seemed in thought for a long time. Then suddenly, she announced loud and clear, "I'll help you."

"You are helping not only me, Lydia, but..."

Lydia cut him off, "I don't know the other people."

Cliff saw the twist in her mind and didn't press further.

Abu and Greg retired to their room. It had two separate beds. That took some of Greg's uneasiness away.

Atta read his thoughts. "Not tonight, Brahim. I guess it's over with. I love you, now, as a brother. We'll die together."

Greg's mind was malfunctioning. "I know that, Abu—so what difference would it make if I had my regular dose of drugs?"

Abu went to the bathroom without responding and took a long pee, then without flushing the toilet, washed his hands and threw a packet to Greg. "The difference is, for me you will never have anything but hate. Same with Lydia. Your love for her takes place only in your imagination."

Without removing any clothes, Greg lay on his bed and relieved his craving. "That's true. Our relationship never worked right within me." He didn't mention Lydia. "If you wanted love you went the wrong way, Abu…like me."

"Brothers in crime," Atta said in his metallic voice. "Neither one of us can escape this brotherhood or go to heaven." He went to the other bed and lay down with his clothes on, too. "Allah never forgets anything. However, if you want to leave, you can walk right out and be blessed."

Now Greg's mind was moving slowly but steadily. Finally, he uttered, bereft of any emotion, "I'll stick with you, Abu."

The next morning Logan Airport's security chief blocked Cliff's emergency plan. Someone from the White House had sent vague and inappropriate orders and informed them that Atta and MacPherson had flown to London. Later, it was found that the tickets were merely decoys. The CIA and FBI had to double check. In the meantime, Cliff and Lydia stayed in front of the security TV monitors all day long.

Nothing. The security officers laughed behind their backs. Lydia retired for the night. Cliff kept his vigil.

The morning of the eleventh of September, agent Cliff rubbed his eyes, he badly needed a break.

"Go get some rest," Lydia insisted. "We'll yell if anything happens."

Cliff retired against his better judgment, rationalizing that he would be of more value with a clear mind.

Lydia sat at the observation post with a young security guard. After a few moments, she sent him for coffee. Did she know what she was doing? Did she realize what was about to take place telepathically? We'll never know...

Was it meant to happen right at this point in time...or no time?

Greg and Abu entered the airline terminal and headed for the departure zone. As Greg passed in front of the TV monitors, he felt Lydia's presence and smiled. In an instant, her face was there imprinted in his mind. Contact had been made.

Lydia was unable to move. Greg was speaking to her in her mind and heart. "I'll always love you darling, but we are going now, Atta and I, to fulfill our separate destinies. You won't betray me, Lydia, will you?"

"Not for anything in this world, my dear." Lydia's lips were moving imperceptibly, trancelike. "I love you, Greg. I won't let you down."

The security guard returned with a carafe of coffee. "Anything new?" he said lightheartedly. "A fresh cup will pick you up."

Lydia didn't answer. She just stared straight ahead in total shock. The guard was confused. He tried to shake her. Should he call a doctor or the agent?

He tried for both. "Uh, sir, you better come see this."

Cliff came running, cursing himself. He shouldn't have left her alone. Had she seen something?

Lydia sat frozen with her eyes glassy and all blood drained from her face, staring at the monitors. Cliff started to make the connection. "What flights are on?" he yelled at the bewildered guard. The guard started to check the departure list.

Greg reached over and grabbed the security phone. "This is Agent Cliff, CIA, give me the Chief of Security, we need to ground all flights immediately."

A mechanical voice came back, "Password please, we don't know you."

Cliff lost control. "Damn it, this is Agent Cliff with the CIA, I'm authorized to talk to the Chief!" He thought to himself, *the lying bastard must have thought this operation a hoax not to have authorized his clearance.*

Abu's false ID had gone through undetected. He walked briskly past the guards. Greg paused for a moment and looked up at the sky-camera and smiled furtively. Like Abu, he was clean shaven, very ordinary, hardly detectable. In the booth, Lydia was still transfixed on the monitors, as airport medics tried to check her.

Cliff was beginning to lose control. He went to another phone and called his boss, to try to convince him that this was a national emergency, as the medics put Lydia on a stretcher. She never moved. They wheeled her away comatose.

But, having seen Abu and Greg pass by undetected, and understanding what they were about to do, Lydia probably intentionally kept her mind a blank. Or was it an act of God? To everyone else, she simply never regained consciousness.

The plane took off smoothly. Greg checked the faces of the ill-fated passengers. They were just faces. Three of them he recognized from the hotel on Monroe Street in Montreal. Two of them were Abu's bodyguards.

Abu watched him intensely. He sat next to him and took hold of his left arm. "What do you feel?"

Greg didn't move. "Nothing."

"Our men are loaded," Abu whispered.

"I'm loaded, too."

Abu's eyes became deadly. "With what?"

"With you and the lives of all these people, maybe more…"

"What are you up to, Brahim?" Abu hissed suspiciously.

"I'm going to help you. I thought that's what you expected of me." Greg spoke evenly, like a talking computer, "I don't know those people. They are nothing to me."

Atta relaxed but not entirely. "We are not going to Los Angeles."

"I know that, Abu," Greg intoned. "A deal is a deal."

Atta was antsy. "I cannot feed you now."

"I don't need a fix," Greg said as he extended his right hand. "No tremor."

Cliff shouted over the phone to his CIA boss, "Stop all take-offs nationwide, ground *all* flights!"

The big man tried to sound mellow, "You did an excellent job, Cliff. Two teams of terrorists have been arrested at Logan. New York is safe."

"I know that, but Atta and MacPherson are still missing."

"Come on, Cliff, you've been notified they are in London—calm down. Scotland Yard will take care of them."

"Those tickets were bought by them as a decoy—no one saw them get off the plane at Heathrow," argued Cliff. "And besides, Lydia has just been in contact with Greg."

"Look, Cliff, we are all in agreement here that your imagination is working overtime. Come back to Washington. You need a rest. We can't shut down airport traffic because of a demented woman's hysteria."

"Look, I'm not a mental case, Boss, you've got to believe me. Let me talk to the President in person."

"Why? I'm writing my report to him. It's an open and closed case. Thanks to you, national security will be raised. Look, your wife is on her way to Boston—she loves you…"

Malarkey, thought Cliff, but his boss went on, "…your wife and daughter need you. So please, don't go to New York, because you'll just raise more havoc. There are already proliferating rumors…"

"What rumors?" Cliff interrupted.

His boss cleared his voice. "That the towers will be hit again."

"That's what I'm telling you—they will!"

Agent Cliff was ready to step on board a flight to La Guardia, New York, when the security chief caught up to him. "We lost control of our flight to Los Angeles. It dropped off our radar."

Cliff paled. "Where?"

"Over Pennsylvania," the corpulent man was breathing hard. "Before we lost it, our operators said the *Boeing* made a wide turn around and this was confirmed."

Cliff knitted his eyebrows. "Let me guess where it was headed. What do you expect from me?"

"This call is for Lydia. I think you should take it." He handed him a cell phone.

"Agent Cliff here."

"I don't want to talk to you. Put Lydia on the phone, I know she's there." It was the voice of Greg MacPherson.

"Lydia has been moved to a hospital, I think she lost the baby," Cliff stated flatly. "What's going on?"

"We have a rough situation. The pilots have been murdered, though Atta still needs me. I'm bleeding, but otherwise okay. All the passengers are in shock, but I'm hoping they will rally against the terrorists…we're close to…" the line faded out then back in, "…the message is, if any jet fighters appear, the airliner will be destroyed. Otherwise, the passengers will be spared…"

"Do you believe it?" Cliff asked sharply.

"Not a bit…tell Lydia I love her. My time has come…" The line crackled dead.

Cliff was stunned. The stewardess asked him, "Are you coming on board, sir?"

The agent came back to his senses and turned to the Chief of Security, "Stop this flight and ground all others. Let's get to the control room. There still may be other hijackings."

The Chief turned to the stewardess, "Mrs. Wigman, disembark all passengers immediately."

The two men moved off toward control.

Two hijackings were aborted in Virginia. The flight to Los Angeles exploded somewhere over Pennsylvania and fell to the earth in pieces. Everyone on board, which included the hijackers, perished.

It was September 11th—9/11.

The media was unusually subdued. Very little was published pending investigation. The President initially had flown away from D.C., then, after hearing from NORAD, Air Force One changed course back to Washington.

In his speech, the President didn't sound subdued. He promised to launch an all out assault on terrorism, but actually felt robbed of his greatest opportunity. He wasn't a patient man and he was going to prove it.

Patience in politics is never appreciated. It's called cowardice. It doesn't work with terrorists either, though they were forced to wait.

For the time being, in this particular dimension, the World Trade Center towers still stood on the forefront of the New York skyline.

For how long was anyone's guess.

Cliff was prevented from seeing Lydia again. Officially she never existed. Ibrahim Ghamal was blown to pieces. The worldwide hunt for Gregory MacPherson was suddenly called off. Nobody missed him anyway. Lydia's mind was blank. In the asylum she went under the name Vegha 77, the only thing she mumbled repeatedly. Her lost baby daughter never entered her deluded mind.

Cliff was given an early retirement with honors. He tried to save his marriage for the sake of his daughter. It didn't work.

He found himself with a lot of free time and little to do. The *odd man out* started writing a *fiction* novel. It took him a long time, but here it is.

PHASE ONE AFTER ZERO

Gregory MacPherson felt nothing, except the animalistic instinct to escape.

Time didn't matter to him, only distance…

About the
Author

Born in Plovdiv, Bulgaria, **Vladimir Chernozemsky** came under intense political scrutiny while working as a documentary director and poet in Sofia. With Communist State Security agents after him for espionage, Vladimir made a harrowing escape to the West. From then on he was constantly on the move — Paris, Rome, Casablanca, Algiers — eventually receiving asylum and citizenship in the U.S.

Vladimir is the author of 46 novels, plays and screenplays written by him in five different languages. For his poems in French he has been praised as "the new Paul Verlaine." He has been hailed for his novels as "an exceptional literary talent" (*MBR/Bookwatch*) and "a talented, accomplished writer" (*Bookviews*). Vladimir is also known for his translations of other works, and as an actor, painter and film/stage director.

He has advanced degrees in Drama/Film from the DEFA in Berlin, Comparative Literature from La Sorbonne in Paris, and Film Directing from Centro Sperimentale di Cinematografia in Rome. He currently resides and works in Los Angeles, California.

Phase One After Zero and other books by Vladimir Chernozemsky are available through your favorite book dealer or from the publisher:

Triumvirate Publications
497 West Avenue 44
Los Angeles, CA 90065-3917

Phone/Fax: (818) 340-6770
E-Mail: Triumpub@aol.com
Web: www.Triumpub.com
SAN: 255-6480

Phase One After Zero (ISBN: 1-932656-03-0)
$22.95 Hardbound.

Dark Side of Time (ISBN: 1-932656-02-2)
Supernatural Fiction, $24.95 Hardbound.

Lion of the Balkans (ISBN: 1-932656-01-4)
Historical War Fiction, $24.95 Hardbound.

A Continent Adrift (ISBN: 1-932656-00-6)
Science Fiction Novel, $24.95 Hardbound.

Please add
$4.50 shipping for first copy
($1.50 each additional copy)
and sales tax for CA orders.